Also by Ann Beattie

WALKS
WITH
MEN

Ann Beattie

Scribner

New York   London   Toronto   Sydney

SCRIBNER

A Division of Simon & Schuster, Inc.
1230 Avenue of the Americas
New York, NY 10020

First Scribner edition June 2010

SCRIBNER and design are registered trademarks of The Gale Group, Inc.,
used under license by Simon & Schuster, Inc., the publisher of this work.

For information about special discounts for bulk purchases,
please contact Simon & Schuster Special Sales at
1-866-506-1949 or business@simonandschuster.com.

The Simon & Schuster Speakers Bureau can bring authors to your
live event. For more information or to book an event contact the
Simon & Schuster Speakers Bureau at 1-866-248-3049
or visit our website at www.simonspeakers.com.

Designed by Carla Jayne Jones

Library of Congress Control Number: 2009052240

ISBN 978-1-4391-7576-7
ISBN 978-1-4391-6869-1 (pbk)
ISBN 978-1-4391-6870-7 (ebook)

WALKS
WITH
MEN

In 1980, in New York, I met a man who promised me he'd change my life, if only I'd let him. The deal was this: he'd tell me anything, *anything,* as long as the information went unattributed, as long as no one knew he and I had any real relationship. At first it didn't seem like much of a deal, but my intuition told me he knew something I didn't yet know about the way men thought—and back then, I thought understanding men would give me information about the way I could make a life for myself. I liked his idea that nobody would know we meant anything to each other: not the college where he taught, or the magazine where he was on staff. Not my boyfriend in Vermont.

"You give me information, and I give you *what*?" I said.

"You give me a promise that nobody can trace anything back to me. I explain anything you want to know about men, but nobody can know I'm the source of your information."

"You think men are that special?"

"A different species. One I understand very well,

because I've sheltered myself there to stay out of the rain," he said. "You're smart, but you're missing basic knowledge that will eventually stop you dead in your tracks."

"Nobody talks to anybody this way," I said.

He said (thumb gently rubbing my wrist): "You don't think I know that?"

Neil had been the writer assigned to provide a perspective on statements I'd made when I was interviewed by the *New York Times*, about why my generation was so disillusioned, but unlike most subjects and commentators, we met. Soon afterwards, he made his offer, and I didn't say no. I was interested. I'd only had two long-term relationships, and I had never had an affair.

We walked in the rain. I wore a Barbour jacket Neil bought for me on Lexington Avenue, in a store on the same block as my hotel. He expressed shock that I, a person of such good taste, didn't already have one. This was the second time we'd met, and it wasn't exactly a romantic occasion. He'd rounded me up at Mount Sinai after I had a laparoscopy. It was a minor procedure: in in the morning, out by early afternoon; apparently, my wooziness and vomiting on the sidewalk had not been anticipated by the doctors because it was not part of the usual scenario. ("A different species.")

Neil and I had first met at lunch, when an editor of the Arts and Leisure section of the *New York Times* suggested the three of us get together (there had been quite a few letters to the editor after my interview, and his "perspective" piece). When he found out I had plans to return to New York later in the month, he insisted on meeting me at the hospital. Afterwards, we took a cab to my hotel and sat shoulder-to-shoulder on the love seat staring into an empty fireplace with a sign above it saying that under no circumstances should the fireplace be lit (did they imagine travelers might get into a snit and destroy old love letters, or that they packed logs?). I felt woozy and headache-y; Neil—who I would soon find out thought often about presents, as ways to cheer people up—started thinking aloud, saying that while I called my mother and stepfather to tell them I was okay, he would go out and get me a better scarf to go with my jacket. What was that nubbly wool thing around my neck? It should be used to buff a car. And wasn't the hotel room drab? ("Never trust a hotel that's been renovated until the *second* year.") Thus began my tutorial: a young woman who'd graduated from Harvard with honors, considering the advice of an older man. The medical procedure had gone well; I was okay, what about a glass of wine (he called it "a drink," and told me that announcing what drink you'd order wasn't done: one always said, simply, "a drink") at the bar downstairs, and then he would tuck me in bed and get me a Burberry scarf—

durable and stylishly understated; good enough for the Queen, it should be good enough for me—and then we could prop up in bed and begin our more serious talk. If I thought of the right questions, he promised to give honest answers, and . . . what? Everything would be known, between someone who was about to turn twenty-two, and the older man she was infatuated with, who was forty-four, all in the honorable cause of the young woman's enlightenment, so she would no longer make the mistakes she had made—might continue to make—if someone (Neil), *the right person*, didn't intervene?

Italics provide a wonderful advantage: you see, right away, that the words are in a rush. When something exists at a slant, you can't help but consider irony.

I became something of an overnight sensation, when I was twenty-one, for an interview I gave the *New York Times*, in which I—one of that year's summa cum laude Harvard graduates—disparaged my Ivy League education, at graduation, in the presence of President Jimmy Carter, and stated my intentions to drop out and move to a farm in Vermont. Neil, a Barnard professor, had been hired to elucidate the issue of my generation's dissatisfaction with the Establishment, writing a piece for the *Times* in which he contextualized my angst by quoting Proust, Rilke, Mallarmé, and Donald Barthelme.

Then—though it had not been implied in the assignment—he concluded the piece by offering me a return to "the old ways," with a facetious proposal of marriage. I dropped him a note when I read it, saying I'd let him know my answer soon. I didn't get it: the ironies within ironies, certainly not the fact that he was only sending up a speculative thought balloon that I mistook for an advertising dirigible.

At the time this relationship began, I had been living in a tiny town in Vermont with a man named Benjamin Greenblatt, who'd graduated from Juilliard and gone to work on a dairy farm, doing chores, growing and canning vegetables, and milking goats to make cheese (a fisherman; a wanderer; a hiker; a sometimes poet; a bass player). By the time I met Neil, though, the novelty of living in the country had worn off, and I was tired of trying to learn to play the pump organ so I could accompany Ben singing lyrics he wrote on napkins and notepads, or took down in shorthand on the palm of his hand. I'd had a yearlong bellyache I didn't think was metaphorical, and had finally been referred by a doctor in Burlington to an OB-GYN (courtesy of my stepfather's intervention) in New York.

The day I met Neil, I had almost signed with a literary agent who'd contacted me after the *Times* piece, and was scheduled, after lunch, to go to the studio of a photographer at the Gulf & Western Building near Columbus Circle. There was instant chemistry between Neil and me, and the presence of the section editor who was with us that afternoon was as annoying as a soggy cocktail napkin. I went to the photographer's studio (the agent wanted me to have good photographs in hand; I didn't think about the fact that she gave me no writing assignment), then met Neil at the place he'd written inside the matchbook: Grand Central. Not anywhere specific, just "G. Central." He did not mention what time I should be there. I imagined he must know how long it would take to be photographed. When it was over, I rode the subway (good instructions from the photographer) and entered the station. I scanned the huge space, then stood by the Information booth, having decided on the most predictable meeting place. Eventually he came toward me, smiling, carrying a bag that held two chocolate cupcakes. The hotel key was already in his pocket.

I was young, and I wasn't used to being secretive with my women friends. Some met us later that week for coffee (I lied to Ben and told him I needed to rest in the city before I could travel). During those hectic few days, my friend Ruby came over to a store where Neil was looking for old jazz albums, and afterwards the three of us went to Washington Square and sat on a bench and drank Cokes. Christa (who had gone to grade school with me and worked for a brokerage firm in the city) went to Mary Boone with us and looked at paintings. Later, when he and I started seeing each other, I found out that the editor who'd been at lunch had called Neil the next day, saying she had an extra ticket to hear Spalding Grey.

"What do you want me to do?" he would eventually say to me, "about your friend X, who called me at work and asked me to have a drink with her?"

He was teaching me even when he was not teaching me.

You make the reasonable assumption that two egotistical people had found each other, shipwrecked like millions of others on the island of Manhattan. It was 1980. Carter was committing adultery in his heart and not getting the hostages freed from Iran, and everyone felt unsettled. The seventies were grinding to a halt like stripped gears. When the talk wasn't about the number of days the hostages had been held, it was about money. Being disenfranchised had about as much cachet as paying for things with cash. Bon Temps Rouler did not exist then—or, rather, it did, though it was not yet the name of a restaurant in lower Manhattan.

To stop me from feeling sorry for myself after the laparoscopy, he pretended the problem was vanity, not pain: "Okay, you have a couple of little marks on your body. Every woman has ear piercings, but you have a belly button that's been stuck, and a tiny scar just where your pubic hair begins." (His finger hovered near the edge of the scar.) "Never act like they're imperfections. They're *who you are*. They let anyone who's lucky enough to see them know that you've been subjected to certain explorations." (He loved stretching out words, mocking them for having so many syllables: "ex-plor-*a*-tions.") "Somebody's examined you the way the Lilliputians looked at Gulliver. The marks are the minuscule footprints left behind."

Also: "Don't use hair conditioner. Electricity is sexy. When your hair falls forward, it reaches out. It lets me know some part of you wants something."

"You have to tell me," I said. "The guy who meets the girl and they have a couple of drinks, maybe only coffee, and he holds her hand as she walks along the curb, she reaches the end and he tightens his grip so she can step down. . . . He's gallantly escorted her, but the next day he doesn't call. He never, ever calls. Explain that."

"Let's say it wasn't a curb she walked along, it was a plank. At the end, he'd *want* to see her walk into the air, wouldn't he? You'd feel the immediacy of that in your gut. If somebody's walking a plank, the only satisfactory outcome is that the person reaches the edge and walks off, and you don't get an *escort* when you do that.

No guy wants to feel like he's the MC escorting Miss America. Listen: if you set out on that walk, then that's your moment. What the *other* person gets is that fabulous, queasy thrill of being with you until the second he has no more control. It's sexual. Understand?"

At night, back in the life in Vermont I was edging away from, Ben Greenblatt sat in his Morris chair with cat-clawed arms, bought at auction for ten dollars, and read Kafka and Borges. Neither of us had real jobs. He made notes in the margins of his precious books. When I eventually snuck a look, I saw there was no punctuation: no exclamation points, no question marks. "Did we already know this," without a question mark, still asks a question, I suppose. But "Foreshadowing catastrophe" without an exclamation point seemed peculiarly anticlimactic.

Ben's mother had worked in a bank; his father, who died when he was twelve, had been a vice president of the bank where his wife worked. He had a sister, Johnlene, who'd been named after both his father and his mother, Arlene. Ben had no middle name. Apparently, his parents felt the previous child already represented both their names, so they hadn't been creative in naming their son. Soon after we broke up, Ben became simply "Goodness." He inherited forty acres of land—as promised, in exchange for chores—when the couple he'd worked for died. The people's son got rid of the goats immediately, sold the remaining half of the land to a developer who eventually built town houses with white exteriors, in a strange configuration that made them look like teeth that needed orthodontia, along with two clay tennis courts and a heated pool. Over the rise, out of view of all this, Ben renovated the old chicken coop and created a yoga studio that was later christened by Pattie Boyd, wielding a bottle of organic cider. This became the famous Goodness Studio, where musicians came to do Downward Dog and the Sun Salutation: a little stretching, post-detox and pre-reunion tour. Bob Dylan himself once showed up during an afternoon session, opened the door, looked at the stunned faces, took off his hat and gave it a Frisbee toss into the studio, then said, "Where there's no dogs, there's no meaningful life," got back in his Jeep, and drove away.

This all happened the year after I left. I heard about it from the postman, who kept in touch with me.

"Ben," I said to him (this was after Grand Central, and after the hospital and the hotel), "I know this is going to be hard for you to believe, but I met a man in New York. He's everything we hate: a professor who sounds professorial; somebody who writes for the mainstream press. But I've fallen in love."

He looked at me for a long time before answering.

Then he said: "Think of me disapproving when he asks you to move to suburbia."

By spring, a book Neil had written, *Prometheus in California: The Rise of the Executive Counterculture,* became the way out of his full-time job at Barnard. Under an assumed name, he also began writing an advice column for a women's magazine, with a panel of so-called experts that included a cross-dressing society haircutter, the owner of a jazz club, and a Ritalin-addicted SoHo veterinarian (his former Harvard roommate). They did it for the way-downtown expense account dinners with Neil, and made a joke of showing up at the restaurant with canned answers, though they didn't know what question would be addressed in the next column. (He brought some letters and got their advice. He spoke to his teenage niece later, on the phone, and asked her to update their response with hip new ways of phrasing things.) With a few minor changes, the answers often worked. I found the literary allusions amusing, the in-jokes droll. He was working on his second book, a novel—though his agent (*my* agent) had urged him to follow up his first book with more nonfiction—and that was the reason he worked in SoHo, in an extra room at the vet's office, his concentration occasionally interrupted by an after-hours emergency. He'd once had to help his friend Tyler wrestle a bloodhound to the floor (forget the examination table) after it had gotten into a restaurant's garbage bag containing the week's coffee grounds. Another time he'd had to give the bad news to the owner of a ferret that had bled to death after being bitten by a rat that had come in through the window. (Tyler had been stoned, had always been phobic about ferrets, and didn't think he could approximate proper sorrow.)

Me? I was doing research at the New York Public Library about birds in the South. (Neil had asked me to. It became a standing joke: how do you hint that someone go to the library and research birds?) I had also researched how moonshine was made, especially inside prisons (even harder to hint at). I had started doing a little freelance copy editing for Neil's book publisher, when I was lucky enough to be called, and I was enrolled in a night school class in essay writing at NYU. I did my research, did my homework, and often went to the movies with friends. Some of them couldn't imagine why I believed Neil was writing every night until dawn. (Because he came back to my apartment. We had early-morning sex. He told me writers wrote at night.)

Other things he told me, that I believed: that you and another person could do something and say the words "This never happened," and it had not happened; that purchasing only the finest brands or shopping

at thrift shops was the only way to acquire things—
anything in between was bourgeois and pathetic; that
only dumb people bought cars instead of leasing them;
crystal wineglasses were for morning orange juice, and
grappa was best sipped from the bottle; Turgenev was a
greater writer than Dostoyevsky; using an exclamation
point for punctuation was interchangeable with eating
food and drooling; Irma Franklin was a better singer
than Aretha. It was morally wrong to buy a purebred
dog.

You see through this; understand I was too naïve,
even if you factor in that I was young. The '80s were not
a time when women had to put up with male tyrants.
No woman had to fit herself around a man's schedule.
To do so was lazy, as well as demeaning. But I didn't
introspect; I didn't ask enough questions. I expressed
passivity by pretending to myself that whatever I did
for Neil was charming, old-fashioned dutifulness.
More embarrassing still was the fact that I let him support me, that I had delusions about becoming a major
essayist (*In this culture?* as Neil would say).

If you think for a minute, you might guess what happened next, because clichés so often befall vain people.

I moved in with Neil. We lived on the fourth floor of
a Chelsea brownstone—a neighborhood Neil loved,

because in those days it wasn't posh and the people who owned businesses were hardworking and polite, helpful and smiling as they greeted customers with their few memorized phrases of English ("Thank you very much" was the owner of the dry cleaner's; "Come back not too early" owned the laundry), and every block had a distinct character all its own.

The people who shared the building with us in Chelsea included a model who lived with a man who wrote for the *Village Voice*; Raymond, a psychologist who saw clients at our brownstone; and the landlord's forty-year-old son, Etch-a-Sketch—as Raymond and I had nicknamed him. Jobless, he, too, often sat on the front steps, fiddling with dials on a plastic box with a pale gray screen on which pictures were created.

One chilly day in June, I was on my way uptown, my fisherman's bag filled with pens and tablets slung over my shoulder, adjusting to my new red Keds, wearing my uniform of jeans and a little cashmere sweater, over which I wore one of Neil's nicely worn, roomy jackets.

Sitting on my front steps was a woman, attractively dressed, clearly not a bag lady or one of the loonies who'd been let out of jail. But who was she who had opened our iron gate to sit on our steps?

She was Neil's wife. She told me in three words.

"Not a clue?" she said. "He was that good at hiding me?"

I don't know what I said. I know that I sat down several steps above her and looked into the trees. The Episcopal seminary was across the street. I looked at that, too.

"We've been in couples therapy," she said, "but it occurred to me today that what he wants to do is marry you—in spite of all the reassurances he's given me that he doesn't—so I thought that for once in my life, I'd try to do the right thing. I thought I'd try to warn you off. Is there any chance you'll listen to me?"

I used the railing to pull myself up and teetered down the steps to where she sat. There was a pack of cigarettes next to her. I looked at the package. It might as well have been my heart.

"He told me I was the exception. That he didn't believe in marriage," I said.

"That's what he told me, too. And as we both see, apparently he doesn't."

"How long—"

"Eleven years," she said. "I lived with him for a while before we got married."

I remembered Neil saying, "People say women are catty, but men are doggy: they just walk around silently with their bone, until they want to bury it."

"I've known about you for months. I should have contacted you sooner. I'm just another one of those wives who go to therapy and meanwhile let their husbands 'work out their problems.' He told me his affair with you would bring us closer. He did! And that we always could have been closer, if I'd been willing to open up to him. You've discovered he likes to give advice? That way he can tell you his opinions and he doesn't have to question himself. Do you know what I did once? I've never told anyone. He had strep throat, and I flushed his antibiotics down the toilet and refilled the bottle with Kaopectate pills. Some part of me really hates him."

"You can have him," I said.

"I thought about getting your number somehow and telling you, but the truth is, I wanted to meet you. You're pretty. I wouldn't have expected otherwise. I'm pretty, too. There we have it."

She took out a cigarette, offered me one, shrugged when I declined, and removed a book of matches from the little purse at her feet, struck one, stuck the cigarette into the flame and watched the flame for a while with crossed eyes, before blowing out the match and inhaling. "I have the same bag you have," she said, on the exhale. "It's the only sensible bag to have, right? The perfect bag."

"How long did you say you'd been married?"

"We don't have children, in answer to your next question," she said. "Eleven years."

"I should have known."

"You should have. Did you really think he was always working?"

"My friends were suspicious."

"My friends hate him, but still: a lot of them fantasize about sleeping with him."

"My friends do, too. They call him. Flirting."

"Then he asks you what he should do about them, right? Letting you know how loyal he is, and at the same time making sure you know how untrustworthy your friends are."

We said nothing for quite some time.

"What's your name?" I asked.

"Lisa," she said. "And of course I'm so enlightened, I keep my maiden name: Lisa Pauline Haley. And you are Jane Jay Costner. *The* Jane Jay Costner. I figure the Jay was your mother's maiden name. Maybe you're Southern, though you don't have an accent."

"You're right, if you consider Washington the South."

"I wouldn't be the first to remark on the number of women writers who have three names, would I?" she said.

"Jane Austen," I said. "George Eliot."

A squirrel went up a tree. A boy walking a beagle yanked its leash, then stopped to watch the squirrel climb.

"Eudora Welty," I said. "Mavis Gallant." I concentrated as if my life depended on it. "Flannery O'Connor," I said. "Alice Munro."

"So here I am, sitting on a step in Chelsea, my marriage done with, and you don't want him, either. It turns out to be his bad day, doesn't it? But there's no spark between us. Am I wrong? I thought if there was, I'd ask you to have coffee."

"Maybe it's jealousy, but I don't really feel drawn to you," I said.

"I have several good friends," she said. "It doesn't matter."

She smoked her cigarette. Next door, a famous actress walked down the steps and headed off for her morning of reading *Variety* and the *International Herald Tribune* at the Empire Diner. One of the waiters told me she brought her own tea bag, and asked for hot water, which they didn't charge her for. Her little dog's paws never touched the sidewalk. She was said to have been a lover of Marcello Mastroianni. She sometimes said hello, but today she didn't. She turned left toward Tenth Avenue.

"I can imagine what the rent on this place must be," she said. "Does he make you pay your share?"

I shook my head no.

"He inherited a house outside San Francisco when his grandfather died. All the legal problems involved, and he never mentioned it. Interesting. Shall I tell you who he rents it to? No curiosity? Well, he can certainly afford the gesture." She dropped her cigarette on the step and moved her foot sideways to squash it. A little puff of smoke rose from beneath her toes and wafted away.

"Where do you live?" I said.

"East Eighty-eighth, off Second. When we got married, we lived in a one-bedroom, then the one next door came up for sale. We borrowed money and bought it, had the adjoining wall knocked out. We gutted the second kitchen. He has a collection of Murano glass in there on glass shelving, with recessed lighting. Below the shelves are his first edition poetry books."

"He's rich?"

"He didn't have as much money as he has now until Edgar died," she said. "That was what—five years ago? I was going to have coffee with you, then go see my lawyer uptown. The subway's not exactly convenient in Chelsea. I took a cab. I'm going to try to get as much of Neil's money as possible. He already hates women, so what the hell. You know that, right? He hates women."

"I guess he does," I said.

"I don't have much of a sense of you," she said. "Are you in shock, or are you a very low-key person?"

"Shock, I think."

"I guess it's possible I wouldn't have known, either, except that we're married. And also, he has such a need to be found out. He's not two-timing both of us with another woman and telling *you* about *her*, is he?" She clasped her hands. "Just kidding," she said. "Oh, you really are *pretty*," she said, standing. She reached down for her cigarette pack and her purse. "Younger than me. Smart. I read that interview with you. Are you giving interviews now? It seems like you shone very brightly for about a week, and then you disappeared."

"Do you hate women, too?" I said. "That's a pretty nasty thing to say."

"The older I get, the less I like people," she said. "You, being my husband's mistress, of course I'd have every reason to dislike."

I looked back at the treetops. The sky was cloudless. In a children's book, one little cloud would skittle across the sky and be a topic of conversation and wonder. The sky was pure blue. As she walked away, a man I didn't know walked down the steps, several stoops away, then turned and went quickly toward Ninth Avenue. I watched him overtake her, and saw her falter. I knew she thought it was Neil, coming up beside her. But it was only a tall man with a briefcase, in a hurry.

You correctly assume that I did not simply leave him. If I had, there wouldn't be much of a story. Not that I stayed for that reason. I stayed because of personal failings. I didn't believe a word of his remorse, I was not moved by his tears, and I told him he was lying when he said he'd been on the verge of telling me. I did not agree to take a walk with him. I took the drink he poured only to say, "This is wine, not 'a drink,'" and threw the glass across the room. I told him to sleep at Tyler's with the rest of the animals, or go back to his wife's. I pointed out that he did not have many friends to call, to ask if they could put him up. Wasn't Tyler his only male friend? And pretty much a loser? When Neil would not leave, I shoved some things in my bag—Kleenex and tweezers and a little box of bitter mints—and walked downstairs to the psychologist's. He was not home, but Etch-a-Sketch was and was gallant about offering me his couch. I was relieved, though surprised, that Neil did not knock on the door.

But he wouldn't do that, would he? So *predictable.* That was bad: to be *predictable.* To walk downstairs, beg. That was for sitcoms, not real life.

Etch had been playing solitaire and drinking Orangina. He produced a blanket from a zippered bag, and a seat cushion he lifted from a chair and slipped into a pillowcase. He folded the blanket in half and tucked the end under the sofa cushion. He muttered, in a worried way, about how bad things happened to everyone. He offered me Tylenol. I took only the glass of ice water. He reassured himself that everything was fine, tomorrow would be another day, such things happened. Then, knowing he'd been talking to himself, he pulled up a chair, as I sat leaning against the back of the sofa, on top of the blanket. He told me that he had gone to D.C. years before, to protest the war in Vietnam, and the person next to him—the guy he'd ridden next to in the bus, and eaten a sandwich with just moments before—had stepped back and doused himself in gasoline and set himself on fire. He cried into his fist, then wiped his eyes and said good night, telling me there were eggs in the refrigerator, if I got up before he did. When he went away and closed his bedroom door, I looked at the clutter on the coffee table. He had a blue Gumby, and he read *The Paris Review*. I kept thinking about Etch-a-Sketch: I've misjudged him, I've brought unhappiness into his life, this is all my fault.

I was conflating my feelings about Etch with my feelings toward Neil.

"*Talk*," Neil said. "When did I ever say *talk* solved anything? It's a device of politicians, to obfuscate. It might be slightly useful for priests who are cornering altar boys. Or to teach a dog its name. *Talk?* That's what's wrong with relationships: we've been made to think we can communicate through talk."

"And your idea is what? To pantomime regret?"

"It's better than talk," he said, dropping to his knees. "If I stay here with my knees digging into the floor, if I kneel until you tell me I can get up, you'll at least have the satisfaction of knowing I've suffered."

"Don't try to turn this around to make me the bad guy. I'm not the one who didn't care who suffered.

I want you to clear your things out of here. You can shuffle around on your knees like some beggar in India while you gather them up. I won't be here to watch it."

He stayed where he was and dropped his head. I picked up my bag and coat and left, leaving the scarf behind, as if it were a dirty tissue.

I was given a key to my friend Janelle's apartment. Except for Wednesdays, when Jan's brother used the apartment to have sex with a wine delivery man who supplied the restaurant next door, the room was mine until she got back from work. Next door, there were cries of passion much of the afternoon. I was amazed at the lovers' ardor, until I finally figured out there was a prostitute in there. In front of the door (which had two peepholes) was a mat depicting Santa and his reindeer, with "Happy Holidays" curving in a long streamer above the sled, from which Santa beamed and waved his black-gloved greeting. Christmas had passed months before. No one was ever in the apartment at night. I tried to be a good guest and changed the water in Jan's flower vase. (I also supplied the flowers.) I vacuumed. The place was so small, there wasn't much to do. I would lie on the couch/bed (covered in the day with an Oriental rug, my sleeping bag shoved underneath) and cry, watch daytime TV, study the Sunday crossword puzzle Jan had already worked, fill in an answer she'd missed, if I knew it, and by late afternoon I would think seriously about getting a job. I provided my own toilet paper and Kleenex. Usually by the time she came home I would have showered, put on under-eye concealer, brushed my hair, and opened the newspaper to a different page than the job listings: the movie listings. The movies were always my treat. She put up with me for about two weeks, then made up the excuse that her brother needed the apartment more often.

She insisted on accompanying me to the Chelsea apartment; she would be protection if Neil hadn't cleared out. When we got there, nothing was gone— had I really expected otherwise?—but there was an envelope for me at the top of the stairs. It contained ten one-hundred-dollar bills, and a note with a phone number: "Have the mover take my stuff to the Salvation Army if you're serious. I'm at Tyler's. I love you."

"He's trying to make you look bad," Jan said. "Manipulative bastard. Why don't you throw a Goodbye, Asshole party? You can pile his stuff in the corner and tell him you had a celebration, instead."

"I've already taken too much of his money. That was my mistake, not to make my own income."

"Oh, I see. You didn't deserve any compensation for being his research assistant and doing all the housework. That makes sense to me."

"I was kidding myself to think it wasn't an issue."

"I'd say that if he can keep two apartments going, and if he tucks a thousand bucks into an envelope, it's not a pressing problem for him."

"Are there any openings where you work? Or do you think I could talk to his publisher and see if they might have anything? I'm going to end up a waitress. I know I am."

"It's New York. Waitresses become famous all the time."

"Name one."

"What's her name, Jessica Lange. Right from the Lion's Head to the fist of King Kong, and the rest is history."

"Are there any jobs open where you work?"

"If it's a serious question, I don't think so."

I walked over to Neil's chair and sat down. "Okay, I'm an idiot, and I feel sorry for myself, and it's my fault I believed him and he's a jerk. But now I have to get out of here, and I'm not going to be able to get an apartment without having a job."

"So get one. You went to college. You're really smart! You're pretty! We'll figure it out. Right now I need some dinner—which I insist he treat us to—and what you need is a pep talk about how everything's not impossible. That'll be easier if I have a couple glasses of wine. We'll go to Claire's. Marvin will send us appetizers and tell us whatever crazy stuff's going on in the kitchen.

You could ask him if he needs a waitress. I'm sure he doesn't, but it might make him think of something."

"You think he might let me be a waitress?"

"Stop it with the waitress tragedy," she said. "It's insulting to waitresses."

"I don't look down on waitresses. I want to be a waitress."

"Let's order a bottle of chardonnay and have a serious talk about how you're done with Neil," she said. "You can bet that egomaniac's sitting across town, tapping his fingers, completely certain you'll show up in SoHo."

Which I did, slightly drunk, about 2 a.m.

The vet's building on Greene Street had been lit up like a place that was expecting me. The second Neil opened the door, I felt the sorrow. It hit me like a cold wind. The people's unhappiness—not his or mine. The sound track was Philip Glass, too loud, and not exactly reassuring music to begin with. There was an eye-wincing smell of disinfectant.

A woman in an evening dress smeared with blood was sobbing in the vet's waiting room, and an older man was patting her hand and holding a whimpering yellow lab on a leash when Neil opened the door. I walked into his arms wearing a raincoat over my nightgown, and high heels I'd mistaken for a pair with lower heels, pulling them out of the closet in the dark. If I'd gone back to change, I would never have continued on. I knew I had to keep going, past Raymond's, past Etch's, out the door, down the steps, into the first cab.

"I know, I know, I know, I know," Neil whispered, cupping the back of my neck and rocking us sideways, forehead-to-forehead. The people looked away. The yellow lab who'd been taking everything in went to the end of its leash, squatted, and peed.

Three months later, after their quickie divorce, we got married at City Hall. I wore a silk, navy blue sheath and a little white stole. He wore a charcoal gray suit with a white shirt and—tucked into the pocket—not a small triangle of scarf, but a piece of handmade paper from Italy, on which he'd written, in gnat-sized handwriting, *I love you,* exactly one hundred times. On the sole of my foot, he had written (while I giggled madly), *She loves me.*

Before we got married, Neil and I broke up after his wife's appearance, got back together, broke up again, got back together, decided to marry, and had a pre-nup drawn up: for every year he didn't cheat on me, or I on him, and I had no reason to divorce him on that account, I would receive $40,000 on December 30, in addition to his paying all our living expenses. If I divorced him for incompatibility, which he agreed not to contest (my lawyer's clause), whether or not I had cheated on him, I would get no alimony, but all my possessions, including cars, jewelry, and other gifts, and a onetime settlement of $50,000. If he cheated on me, I would get the same cars, jewelry, and other gifts and, as a lump sum, fifty percent of his net worth, on which he would pay the taxes (my lawyer). This pre-nup would be "revisited" after five years, though no sums could be negotiated downward and would have to take inflation into consideration (my lawyer). I agreed not to bear children. He had a vasectomy. When we got married we bought ourselves armloads of flowers at our favorite Korean grocer and went home to drink Prosecco. My friend Christa made us a wedding cake without tiers (embarrassing) and fresh raspberries rolling around the big round plate like marbles. My stepfather, Carl West, flew in for the party we had that night, but my mother—big surprise—was too hungover to come. Neil's uncle and niece—the one much-consulted on the telephone about his column—were there from Port Washington, having brought uninvited guests named the

Perrys. Jan did not come, though she'd promised that she would try. Instead, a FedEx letter from her was delivered the next day, telling me I was an idiot with no tendency toward self-preservation. That weekend a reception was held at Neil's uncle's house in Pennsylvania, which had a private landing strip and underground firing range, and a lot of enormous men walking around with walkie-talkies, who seemed very amused by the notion that they were in the movie business. They drank whiskey instead of champagne and slammed their fists into each other's biceps, calling each other "Producer."

Jan made clear that she thought I was living with the devil. We agreed not to talk about Neil, but he kept coming up in her conversations during the next few weeks, and finally I stopped calling her. It was really too much that she thought the yellow lab who had died at the vet's the night Neil and I reunited had been an omen of bad things to come.

Neil was good to me. One condition for staying with him had been that he had to promise that the tutorial was over. If he started in with wise advice, I walked out of the room. He gave up writing at the vet's in SoHo and rented a different place in the East Thirties in someone's illegal B&B. He hired a male graduate student at CCNY as his research assistant. His next book was a huge success. His editor gave a party on the roof of his apartment, with a classical guitar player and all the Veuve Clicquot you could drink (glass flutes, not plastic.) Viva was there, and Eddie Fisher. Woody Allen came, but turned around in the lobby and left (according to the doorman). The *Village Voice* writer, David Fegin, came, though he no longer lived in our building, and the model he'd been with had married an Arab. Fegin arrived with Harold Brodkey, who insisted almost immediately that they leave, because of the noise.

I had some good luck at the same time Neil published his next book. My agent called, saying I'd been asked to work as a script doctor on a documentary filming in New York about runaways. It was called *Chaff*, and it turned out the director liked my writing so much, he had me take it from the top and rewrite the entire voice-over. I went to Times Square, I managed to get access to a few people in drug rehab programs (though it wasn't officially allowed—David Fegin was a help), I talked to psychiatrists, hung out in Washington Square Park. I had a Deep Throat on Avenue A who set me straight about some of the stories I'd been told. The movie won an Academy Award the following year for Best Documentary, and my name was the first thing out of the director's mouth when he ran onstage. If you've heard of me, that's probably why—not many people remember the earlier interview I responded to sincerely, as if I were the first person to uncover the tediousness of academe, back when I thought any of my opinions mattered.

"Forgiveness," Neil said, drawing out the three syllables. "What does that mean, for*give*ness? That life's a storybook, and somebody has been drawn as a queen, sitting on her throne with a scepter, ready to sprinkle forgiveness on her humble servant—that short little bent-over man, the other person in the picture—for tripping on the carpet?"

"Maybe the humble servant trips because he's nervous that she might know he's an adulterer."

We were "taking it easy." Going to the Gramercy Park for "a drink." Thinking about whether we wanted to be together again.

The cabdriver's eyes flashed in the rearview mirror.

"We'll make it a pop-up book," Neil said, lowering the voice the way he did when he was talking to himself, *sotto voce*. He wanted to give the impression that his imagination was so powerful, he got lost, himself, when he began to speculate. "The queen jumps up. She waves the scepter, but no stars sprinkle out. All the stars have dried up, like ink in a pen. Oh, no! What happens to her now? She's got no more magic."

"Maybe she doesn't need magic. Maybe she can just tell him to leave."

"We've been over this before," he said, squeezing my hand. "You don't want me to leave. You're worried about what people think—you're worried about what people you don't even know think. Icarus falls, and they don't look up."

The cabdriver did not slow down for a deep pothole. My teeth vibrated. Neil let go of my hand, trying to stabilize himself by pushing against the Plexiglas divider. Again, I had seen the cabdriver's eyes in the rearview mirror, and also his mouth, with its flicker of disdain.

In Washington Square, a man with a heavy accent stood ranting on top of a plastic crate turned upside down, vegetables trailing out of it like a gigantic umbilical cord. "Sixty-six hostages taken. Six six six is the mark of the Devil. They are the Carter Devil's countrymen, taken right from the American Embassy, not protected, not rescued because Carter Devil wants them prisoners! People unite! Now all know Carter is the Devil!"

"Where are the Maysles brothers when we need them?" Neil said, tugging on my sleeve. "Come on, next the Protestor Devil passes the hat. Or his horns. Maybe next he grows horns and upends them, and we drop our money inside."

"I couldn't understand what he was saying."

"You thought if you stood there longer it would be clarified? *I love you.*"

Sailors know to train their eyes on the horizon to avoid seasickness. When you're landlocked in New York City, look at the farthest curb, which, in its own way, is the horizon line.

Carl West, my stepfather, called to say that in the summer, he and my mother would be taking a cruise to Alaska. He hadn't seen *Five Easy Pieces*, didn't get it when I imitated the deep-voiced woman hitchhiker, who told Jack Nicholson: "I've seen pictures that indicate to me that it's very clean." Then, unexpectedly, he invited me on the cruise. "We don't see much of you," he said. "Maybe a trip would be a way to spend some time together. Just the three of us," he quickly added.

"You're not inviting Neil?"

"Your mother thought that the three—"

"My mother doesn't approve of Neil because of his age. And because he's divorced. It's irrelevant that she's divorced. What if I didn't approve of you because you leave stubble when you shave?"

"I do?"
Alaska!

Two years after I left him, Ben Greenblatt stood in the hallway of the Chelsea apartment, carrying brochures advertising a meditation center about to open in York-ville.

"More yoga in New York? Isn't this a bit like letting people in Moscow know that an ice rink will be open-ing soon in Siberia?" Etch wanted to know.

Ben's hairline had severely receded; now he had a ponytail and wore glasses. He had on a worn T-shirt with a photograph of the Dalai Lama screened on the front. The shirt hung loosely, making the Dalai Lama's face look jowly. The sleeve of the shirt showed a yin-yang emblem. He was wearing thick white socks with dirty toes and threadbare heels, Birkenstock sandals, and black cotton pants with a drawstring waist. He was talking earnestly to Etch, in the entranceway.

"I don't know, man, I get in trouble for taking in flyers from Chinese restaurants and that's something the tenants want to order, you know?" Etch said as I entered the corridor.

Ben looked past Etch. I was sure I was going to be shot in the brownstone in which I lived. He raised his hand, holding brochures, and said only: "I knew you lived here. I am not going to insist upon speaking of spiritual enlightenment, or anything that would cause distress. Namaste. I offer a greeting of friendship, between two individuals who have shared happiness, and who have had the gift of being long acquainted."

"Holy shit, he knows you?" (Etch, too, was thinking: *Valerie Solanas.*)

The hall table, where brochures and the mail were left, was empty except for a marble obelisk. Ben carefully placed the brochures on the table. "A surprise, I'm sure," he said. "I was visiting a friend. A seminarian. Across the street. I'd seen you through the gate, another time I was visiting. I wish no one any harm," he said, picking up on Etch's fear.

"He was my boyfriend," I finally managed to say.

"Wow, your choice in men," Etch muttered, and quickly retreated to his apartment.

"Oh, Ben," I said.

"I was unsure of the right thing to do. I spoke to Rama, and he said that of course I must greet you and wish you well. It is when we carry bad feelings that we, ourselves, are diminished. Do I recall that this line of inquiry was not interesting to you? I wonder, though, whether, for old time's sake, we could spend a few moments together to acknowledge and honor our past?"

"Come upstairs, Ben. I'll make you some tea," I said. "I'm sorry not to have offered. This is rather . . ."

"Goodness," he said, smiling.

It took me a few seconds to realize that he was not commenting, but correcting me about his name. "Goodness?" I repeated.

"Let me get you something at the Empire Diner," he said. "People like me don't take a vow of poverty, you know. I'd be happy to treat you to a cup of tea, or—"

Etch opened his door, then quickly closed it again.

"My friend's a little jumpy," I said. I thought about mouthing "Vietnam," but did not. We went out the front door, down the steps, through the gate, onto the sidewalk.

"Do you still have the farm?" I said.

"I sold the land to an organic farmer from South Dakota and his wife and two daughters," he said. "My friends Amah and Rowinda. Their daughters' names are still evolving."

"But what about—"

"What has come to pass has come to pass. The goats have gone on to other farms, and it was the destiny of Amah to marry, and to live off the land."

"I don't think I'm going to be able to have a conversation with you if you keep talking this way," I said.

"I have transcended anger."

"I know, but you must remember the way you used to talk. Can we just talk that way, instead, so we can communicate?"

"Can you see that my hands hold no answers?" he said, turning out his palms.

We went into the Empire Diner and sat at a booth. The famous actress was talking to a man in a black cloak. For a minute I thought he might be a priest, then saw his motorcycle boots and decided not.

"What can I get you?" the waiter said.

"Iced tea, please," I said.

"Two," Goodness said.

"Thanks for not telling him you wanted some golden lemon blessed by the sun's rays," I said.

He frowned, but turned up his lips at the same time. "Encompass the reality of others," he said quietly.

"You're not going to tell me what you've been doing, why you're in New York, what happened to the farm?"

He squinted through his glasses. "I can't believe you care," he said.

"Also, your voice is a whole octave higher."

"Not eating meat."

"You're putting me on."

He shook his head. "No. No, giving up meat raises not only the spirit, but the voice."

"You're regressing," I said. "You were doing better when you accused me of not caring."

"Here you are, two teas and"—the waiter dipped to pick up the sugar dish from the counter and placed it prettily between us—"anything else? Before you leave my huge tip, I mean." He laughed at his own joke. He'd waited on me before, though we hadn't yet struck up an acquaintance. I thought being there with Goodness might set that agenda back a bit.

"I thank you for bringing the slice of lemon, blessed by the sun's rays," Goodness said.

The waiter looked back at the table. "Is that an allusion to something?" he said.

"Neil," I called into the bathroom. "Remember my old boyfriend, Ben, from Vermont?"

"I never met him."

"No. But he's in the city now. He came by with pamphlets about a meditation center he and some woman are opening."

"Did he declare his undying love? Wait! He was the one who wrote you that letter and said you were a ball-buster, right?"

"Right."

"And?"

"Well, just that it was strange to see him. He said he'd seen me once before, when he was on this block. I kept thinking he'd drop the peace and love routine, and he did sort of falter, but then it went back to being impossible. We were at the Empire. All the waiters hint for big tips now, and pretend they're being ironic."

"I noticed that."

Neil came out of the bathroom with a towel wrapped around his waist, a smear of shaving foam near his ear. "The new showerhead doesn't have any middle range," he said. "But I'll be damned if I'm prying it off and installing another one. Is this the windup for the pitch? Goatboy wants you back?"

"He doesn't want me back," I said, zipping my dress without having to ask for help. "Some guru's living inside him like a tapeworm, excreting peace and love. They do that, you know. Tapeworms shit."

"No more sushi," he said, opening the closet door.

"You have something invested in thinking I'm more desirable than I am."

"Etch carries in the groceries and painted the kitchen because you batted your eyes at him."

"He used to be a housepainter. He doesn't want to be retired. He's just cracked up."

"He doesn't like me."

"Well, no, he's not crazy about you. But you prefer the attention of women, anyway."

"Yeah," he said, straightening his tie. "What do you want me to do about Sharon Stillerman, calling me at work to ask how we like the BMW we're leasing? She couldn't ask you how we liked it?"

"Maybe she thought you could tell me she called and make me feel insecure."

"Sharon's flirtatious."

"Yes, but she doesn't want anything."

"Oh, really? So if I call back and ask if she wants to take a test drive, that's fine with you?"

"If you'd rather we stay home and have sex, just say so."

"What?"

"This is a game you play to pump up your ego. If you and Sharon, with her big front teeth and her crepe-y eyelids, are going to have an affair, there's nothing I can do about it."

"Put your coat on. This is *before* you have a drink?"

"Right: honest woman as bitch," I said, putting on my coat.

I whispered to Neil in bed sometimes, not wanting to get up, whispering because he whispered: "In the afterlife, there are only pencils, no pens. And every pencil has an eraser."

That one really made him smile, I saw, as I lifted my lips from his ear. He knew I was mocking him for his epigrams, but still: it was Sunday morning, we'd slept late, and he was amused.

"Clouds are poems, and the most moving poems linger on the blackboard so long, written in cursive so lovely, they also exist inside our fingertips. We never really erase them at the end of the lesson."

"You've got a perverse talent for this," he said.

"Picasso used to pick up babies and hold them in front of the camera like a human shield. He would have seemed crazy, except that he was Picasso, so of course someone was looking through a lens."

"I don't get it."

"If you're famous, the world follows you. All you have to do is take care not to pull arms out of sockets."

"It was his son."

"He also played with the children of Gerald and Sara Murphy."

He turned over. "Think of all the things I've taught you," he said.

He taught me to think about the world as if I were contemplating it from the perspective of a figure in a Hopper painting. Maybe the collie. He gave me an ice pick, one time, and put an ice cube on the breadboard and set in front of me a photograph of Bernini's *Daphne and Apollo*. He told me what synesthesia meant, and gave me a wonderful Italian perfume made with lemon verbena that he taught me was sad. Before I met him, I'd never heard of osso bucco, and I would never have made the analogy between eating bone marrow and having a religious experience. Also, he was right about having flashlights. (I loved the bouquet of flashlights sitting in a vase, aimed at the ceiling when we made love. The shadows we cast over our heads.)

"I did a good job," he said.

"You did, but you made me an outsider, and now I'm

stranded, except for you. There's no one else I can talk to about these things and what they mean."

Watch children, to remember how to play.

If you take food home from a restaurant, don't say it's for "the dog." Say that you want the bones for "a friend who does autopsies."

Valentine's Day is for suckers. Buy *real* lace, and think of something else to do with it.

Never wear a T-shirt advertising a place in that place.

Asparagus are the best vegetable, but never trim the ends; people cut the fat off steak, don't they?

Esther Evarts was really Sally Benson—get old *New Yorkers* and read her.

Look at the Riviera, look at Matisse, look at the Riviera again.

I saw it on the TV news just a week or so after seeing Ben. A man had been pushed under a train coming into the Union Square station. A black woman in a turban was telling the TV reporter about how she tried to stop the pusher, sticking the point of her umbrella in his ribs, when she realized what was about to happen. "Yeah, you just got seconds to try to prevent something, you-know-whud-I-mean?" a young man was saying. "You-know-whud-I-mean?" He was with the woman—her son? A friend? She had the umbrella in hand again, and said that if it had happened at night, she'd have had Mace. "You don't got but seconds, you-know-whud-I-mean?" the man was saying again. A man in the background bobbed behind their heads, making a heart sign with his fingers and mouthing someone's name. Another camera got rid of him, focusing from a side angle on the woman and the man beside her.

It was Goodness. Ben, who'd been pushed under the train. An old photograph I recognized as his passport photo was flashed on the screen. The mayor, outside Gracie Mansion, was saying that such actions would not be condoned. More police would be sent into the subways. The dead man was a "humanitarian who offered kindness to many and came to New York City hoping to improve the quality of our lives." A woman weeping in the crowd was identified as one of the mayor's secretaries. She'd taken yoga classes from Goodness. The passport photo had disappeared from the screen, and there was footage of Ben—Goodness—wearing a party hat, blowing out a candle. I'd just been able to make out the top of the Dalai Lama's head on the shirt he wore. The shaky amateur video ended. The mayor answered a reporter's question by saying that more police would be sent into the subways. Someone had taken the mayor's elbow and he'd turned away. The secretary could be seen, not quite off-screen, crying.

I'd tried to breathe normally, the way anesthetists tell you to breathe when they clamp a plastic cup over your nose. I had almost been able to feel phantom hands hovering around my head. The news continued. Someone who owned a bodega had been arrested for selling controlled substances hidden in the bottom of devotional candles.

I went into the bathroom and ran water in the sink, splashed some on my face, but made a mess. It streamed down my arms. I closed the toilet lid and sat down. Would it have been a greater shock if we hadn't seen each other again, or was it less of a shock because I'd seen him? At least I'd known he was living in New York. But where in New York? Near the meditation studio? Near Union Square?

Pushed under a train. The person who had names for his goats, made cheese, and grew herbs. Such a nice person, the people who hired him left him half their property when they died. I'd gone to New York City and taken up with the first person who came along. How could that have been true? What happened to the things I left in Vermont? What book had I been reading that I'd left behind?

I thought about it, and did not call Neil, but looked for the number of one of the doctors I interviewed when I was writing the *Chaff* script. I had talked to him, a forensic psychiatrist, in his office on Park Avenue. I still had his card. I still had everyone's card in a big box. Just a few days before, Neil had been rummaging for the name of the plumber. Had Ben lived not far away, near the Union Square stop? Did he have something romantic going with the mayor's secretary? What was wrong with me—did I think only romance counted? What kind of a romantic life did I suppose I was leading? I remembered that the doctor contacts were all together, a rubber band wrapped around them. And then I remembered his name, and realized I could call Information. The thought was at first exhilarating, then daunting. How would I explain why I was calling? What book had I been reading before I left Ben, in Vermont—something I'd been very involved in . . . an essay? I'd been frustrated not to be able to continue, meant to buy another copy of the book, but never had. At least, I could not remember that I had. There had also been a green sweater.

I remembered coming back to the apartment with Jan, finding the envelope with the message he was at Tyler's and the money. What had once seemed an astonishing amount of money. Everything might have been otherwise, if I'd listened to her. She had talked to me so earnestly at dinner about leaving Neil. She'd had faith in my ability to get a job. To do most anything. She'd made me promise I would call the mover the next day. I had walked around the apartment, gone to bed, gotten up again, put on my spike heels and pulled a raincoat over my nightgown and taken a cab to SoHo.

That was where I would begin with the psychiatrist. I would explain who Neil was. That I'd left Ben. First, of course, remind him who I was.

Instead, I called Jan and got her machine. I said, "You were right, I made a big mistake about how I handled things with Ben, and I drove a decent man crazy, I'm sure I did, I promised I'd be with him forever, and he was hit by a train. He's that man. I know you saw it on the news. Jan, I'm sorry for not being nicer, for putting you in a position where you had to give me advice, then blowing you off. I stayed at your apartment too long, I know it. Neil has never hurt me, you were wrong about that. He can be a mind-fuck, but he doesn't have a violent bone in his body, unlike some maniacs. I really resented your not coming to the party after we got married, but you were doing what you thought was right, I know that. Okay. Bye."

The TV screen was dark, though I couldn't remember having turned it off. The remote control switch had been missing for days. I was sure I'd gathered it up when I'd taken the sheets to the laundry. I should walk to the corner, pick up the sheets, hope that the remote would be there. Instead, I phoned Dr. Fendall and left a message on his answering machine. Almost immediately after I hung up, the phone rang.

"Ms. Costner? Dr. Fendall. I could tell from your message that you're distressed. Do you think you'd be able to come to my office if I send a cab to your address?"

"Well, yes," I said. "I'm not doing anything."

"Good," he said. "You're still on West Twentieth? Let me put you on hold for one moment to call a cab, and then you and I can continue talking."

"I'm a little shaken up. A man I used to live with jumped in front of a train today. I mean, he didn't jump, he was pushed."

"Putting you on hold for just a brief moment," Dr. Fendall said. Muzak began playing: "Raindrops Keep Fallin' on My Head." It took me back to the rain, the walk with Neil, when I hardly knew New York, that bizarre woman sitting on our front steps, exuding hostility, and then her lawyer's incessant phone calls about money.

At Dr. Fendall's office, the first thing he told me was how relieved he was to see me; he'd been almost certain that after he'd called the cab, I wouldn't still be on the line.

Neil had been in Boston that day. He'd left from LaGuardia before I woke up, and would be back that night. We weren't the sort of couple who checked in with each other during the day. He was interviewing someone at MIT for his new book and having dinner with his old friend Turaj. Dr. Fendall knew my address because he'd kept my business card, too. I suddenly remembered that the book I had been reading in Vermont had been by a man named Perrin, who lived there and farmed his land. I had had a lot of success, quite young, and then had lost my way. My relationship in Vermont was not satisfactory, in large part because I knew I should be doing more meaningful things. The man I lived with—Ben—had been angry, and what he'd done was mount a pretty ineffectual protest whose primary goal was to make himself more or less disappear.

"You did not have similar views about life?" Dr. Fendall asked.

It was true: I had not personally valued the things he valued. He had been a promising musician (bass: Juilliard. A talent with wind instruments, as well). On occasion, I used both marijuana and cocaine, but drugs did not contribute to my problem. I could usually get to sleep. No—alcohol was not something I thought about before turning in.

"And who is the source of these drugs?"

A veterinarian in SoHo, who seesawed between Ritalin and Seconal, himself. Yes, he was successful. To my knowledge, no one had reported him for anything. My much older husband was in Boston. "Much older husband" made me giggle. Yes, the old man sometimes took drugs with me, but no, neither one of us had ever gone to bed with an alcoholic beverage on the night table. What was so funny? Well, just the *idea* of being addicted. Me and some old man. I did consider it a happy marriage. We both liked our work, which was similar enough and dissimilar enough that we could bounce ideas off each other and have interesting conversations and not feel like we were invading the other's territory. *Chaff* was a title decided on by the director of the movie. It really *was* a good documentary. The last time I had used drugs? About a week ago, watching daytime TV: a rerun of highlights from *The Ed Sullivan Show*. I did not consider myself depressed. Lazy, sometimes. I'd left the sheets at the laundry for days, but we had more sheets. Not even calling to see if they had found the remote, though, was lazy. Oh, to me it meant just not getting it together to do much of anything. Headaches were not a problem. Oh, *that day,* sure—but not usually. Neither I, nor my old husband, wanted children. He'd had a vasectomy. A pre-nup was what I meant by "contract." Since it seemed to be to my advantage, what the hell. I had, indeed, thought to get my own lawyer. I sometimes listened over and over to a tape of "We Are the World" and tried to figure out whose voice sounded like a knife slicing the air. I wouldn't do any more research for Neil after I found out he was married. She was younger than he, but older than I. Thirty-five? Maybe older, but she still looked good. I had just seen her that one time. She had been on her way to a lawyer's. I did notice that people seemed very uninhibited about what they said to me. I would have no trouble believing I was giving out some signal I wasn't aware of, but what might it be? Recently, it seemed fewer and fewer people talked to me. My friends in the apartment building did, but the psychologist had gotten an office a few blocks away, and Etch, the landlord's son, had come out of the closet, and for a timid person, some of the people he brought in were downright scary.

"Could we return to Ben and to your relationship?" Dr. Fendall said.

The relationship I'd had in Vermont had lasted a little less than a year. I had been young. I wasn't old, *like my husband,* but looking back, Ben and I had been a couple of kids. Marijuana, but no other drugs. My husband thought psychiatrists were witch doctors, and I understood that was defensive. Or arrogant. It was important to him to give the impression he knew things. Important things underlying the things that were verbalized. In the summer Neil and I would be freeloading off some people who'd chartered a yacht, sailing to the Greek Islands. Drugs might or might not be aboard. It would be inappropriate to try to contact the mayor's secretary if all I really wanted to know was if she and Ben had had a romantic relationship. My husband liked to do things spontaneously—have some fun. He was smart, and he had a good sense of humor. Something of a mystery to me. Well: better someone be mysterious than that the mystery be solved, because you might be stuck with an answer you didn't want. I would not say that I asked many questions. Yes, he would probably have considered that nagging.

"What were his thoughts on Ben?"

Wouldn't any response to that be sort of like *He knows that she thinks that he doesn't understand, and she knows that he knows that that's true, but what he and she don't know is that their plane is going down?* It's sort of a game: something you'd see in a comic strip, in the bubble above the dog's head. I couldn't repeat it; it was just doggerel. A pun! Doggerel! Which certainly *did* take us far from the initial question.

If it had been a movie I could edit, this is the way the new version would go:

Neil's wife wore jeans, which fit her well, and flat shoes, which were then so unfashionable, they were fashionable. She smoked Benson & Hedges. There was a book of matches . . . what restaurant's logo? Shoulder-length hair. She wore a gold wedding band. She hadn't gone running out of her Upper East Side apartment without giving thought to how she looked. She said: "I imagine that you knew without knowing. Don't you think that's true?"

"Hi, excuse me, I'm in the middle of an emergency," Raymond, the psychologist, said, opening the gate and sprinting up the steps. I heard his key opening the front door. Her feet were pressed together. My world was about to change. Some poet . . . Rilke. Rilke had been all for that. Easy for someone else to say that you should change your life. "To be honest, it would be better if you weren't sitting here ten minutes from now. I'm expecting someone who's having a very bad day," Raymond called over his shoulder. The door closed behind him.

"He has patients," I said to her.

"He seemed quite impatient."

"No, he's a shrink. Psychologist, I mean."

"Oh. I thought you and I just had very different perceptions."

"You can have him," I said. "I don't want someone who deceived me."

She ran her hands down her jeans, though they fit her too tightly to have wrinkles.

"My friends were suspicious," I said, wishing my voice had come out louder. I wasn't sure how much longer I could talk. "My friends call him, flirting. I guess he's vain because he has reason to be."

"Does he ask you what he should do about them? Like it's your problem? He wants you to think you don't have real friends. That way he gets more power over you."

There was the seminary across the street. The trees. The same view I looked at every day. Her ring sparkled less when the sun went behind a cloud. Thereafter, the cloud drifted away, and the sky was blue and empty.

"What's your name?" I asked.

"You're like him, aren't you?" she said. "Very tentative about asking a question. Like the question mark's going to get airborne and stick its hook between your eyes."

We were looking at each other.

"Lisa," she said. "And of course I'm so enlightened, I keep my maiden name. Lisa Pauline Haley. And you are Jane Jay Costner. *The* Jane Jay Costner. I saw your movie after it won the Academy Award. You're pretty and young and talented. My guess is that Jay was your mother's maiden name. That you're Southern. Maybe." She shook her head. "So I'm sitting on a step in Chelsea, finally done with my husband, and now you don't want him either."

She thought she knew everything. She was a version of him. What if I *did* want Neil? There'd be no reason to tell her, even if it was true.

She said: "Well, it turns out to be his bad day, doesn't it? But there's no spark between us. Not him and me—me and you. Am I wrong? If there was, I'd ask you to have coffee."

"You're right. I don't feel at all drawn to you," I said.

"Maybe it's jealousy. I have several good friends. It doesn't matter."

A boy who had already walked his beagle one way

turned and walked in the other direction. I'd never seen the boy or the dog before. I'd heard that James Earl Jones lived on the block, but I'd never seen him, either.

"Did he brush your soft earlobes with his lips, lower his voice to a whisper, nearly hypnotize you? We'd lie in bed almost nose-to-nose, and he'd ask me to recite passages he'd had me memorize. Shakespeare's sonnets. I'm sure you and I could recite in unison."

I shook my head no.

"I don't believe you," she said. "Cigarette?"

I shook my head no again.

"You know, if he came along right this minute, he'd try to signal both of us, secretly, that we were the one," she said.

I was trying to breathe normally. Had I known without knowing? Would she ever go away? "He washed your hands, didn't he? You couldn't lie about that. You'd be standing at the sink and he'd come up behind you and pick up the soap and lather his own hands, clasp your little hands in his, and rub them while you laughed. It was a turn-on, wasn't it?"

"You can have him," I said again. "He's all yours."

"You really never thought he might be leading a double life? I guess it's possible I wouldn't have known, either, except that we were married. And also, he had such a need to confess. Did he love you, did he just desire you, did he *not even* desire you? I'm telling you

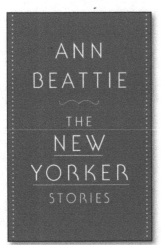

as . . . I was going to say 'friend,' but I'm not your friend. We haven't hit it off. Let's say I'm speaking as his ex-wife. What he understands is money. Protect yourself and make sure you end up with that, if it doesn't work out." She looked at me. "I have the same bag," she said. "He convinced two smart women that purses were embarrassing, but carrying a bag Englishmen fill with trout isn't."

Etch and his boyfriend, Kim, got excited if someone watched while they had sex. Kim burned incense and walked around vamping in a white silk robe he'd shoplifted. Then there was the box. The box was a large framed screen, about the size of a television, with wheels. Kim kept it in the closet and took it out when they had sex, tugging it along with a rope. He spent some time angling it exactly the way he wanted it, facing the bed. When it was turned on, the sound system blared the noise of a storm, and lightning flashed across the sky. Apparently, it had once been used in some puppet show. I found it bizarre—more intimidating than a real thunderstorm.

This spectator sport was something I'd started doing once or twice a week, as the sun began to set: sharing a joint, having a glass of wine with Etch and Kim, looking out the window while they undressed (an odd bit of propriety: I'd wait until I heard Etch get into bed, then watch while Kim slowly took off his robe and did his little undressing dance). I sat in the corner chair (discarded, one night, by the famous actress, snapped up immediately by Etch) to watch. The box's storm was a little too theatrically noisy to be scary, but it wasn't quite funny, either. The strange thing was that other times, when real thunder rumbled, I always thought of the box and burst into laughter. Kim was a dancer, so the sexual pyrotechnics were often quite impressive. But I also became fascinated with the way his white robe pooled on the floor, thinking that if I knew how to take photographs, I could have quite a collection of images. The robe had real personality.

Then, around six, Etch showering, Kim sometimes sleeping, sometimes pulling on the robe, I'd wander out without saying goodbye and find myself ascending the stairs as if the climb was out of my control—just something that happened. And then, a little exhausted myself, I'd make a reservation for dinner, or think about going out to the Korean grocer, what I might buy there, what I might cook.

Neil and I stood at the red light.

"Negative Capability: 'When a man is capable of being in uncertainties, mysteries, doubts, without any irritable reaching after fact and reason.' You've got to love Keats. Forget his figures on the urn. He's using the word *irritable,* as if facts should make a person *irritable.*"

Rollerina streaked by, curving into Washington Square Park: a guy on skates, in a ballgown.

The light turned green.

One of the runaways who'd been in *Chaff* got in touch with me through my agent and invited me to her high school graduation. She was going to start school at NYU in the fall. She'd been diagnosed as bipolar, and being on medicine was a miracle. As an infant, she'd been sold at a shopping center in Paramus, New Jersey. The adoptive parents had had to pay the teenagers (her parents) in deutschmarks. This had all been facilitated by an ex-nun who worked for a phony Catholic organization funded by the CIA. And that was just the beginning.

On the telephone, I told her I didn't like ceremonies, but I was proud of her, and would like to take her to lunch. She named the restaurant, and the date. It was an Italian restaurant on Mulberry Street, Via. Her name was Destiny.

She'd made a reservation: "Destiny, for two." She'd matured into an attractive girl with high cheekbones and an aquiline nose who might have been a model if she'd grown taller. She was still very thin, her cuticles still bitten, her nails ridged. She'd been in rehab and ordered bottled water with a slice of lemon. I ordered the same.

"One big bottle's better," the waiter said, walking away.

It turned out lunch was free, because the owner's daughter had gone through rehab with Destiny; they'd been roommates, and the daughter felt Destiny was responsible for turning her life around. She didn't come to lunch because she was nine months pregnant and couldn't walk.

"You never told us about you," she said. "I guess it didn't matter, but we were always so curious. About anybody who wanted to hang out with us who seemed okay, I mean. We'd decided we could do without most adults."

"Yeah, it didn't seem proper, or whatever word I'm looking for," I said. "I'd never done anything like that before. I happened to have the good luck to be called in to fix a script, and Larry was so impressed he let me completely rewrite it."

"When it won the award, I peed my pants," she said.

"So you're doing it yourself, huh? Going to study film? And I'm so happy about your graduation."

"Thanks," she said. "I think a lot of us would like to get in touch with you, but maybe a few of us aren't doing so well, or they didn't necessarily finish school, and sometimes it makes them think they're not, you know, somebody you'd feel good about seeing, even though they're not still messed up, really. June Bug still is."

"Well, I hope they realize they can contact me if they want to. Is there someone in particular you're thinking of?"

"No. Just, you know, some of them. You were a big hero to us. Getting us to talk about our reasoning. I mean, how cool is it that it won the Academy Award?"

"Incredibly cool."

"We had this fantasy life about you. We weren't all hanging out together or anything—we didn't even all know each other—but when we did meet, at that party at that place in Brooklyn? The girls were saying you were going to tell us about your life. That you'd been a druggie, or one of them thought you'd been raised in a convent."

"Neither thing is true," I said.

"I still see Blake and Sharon. She has a picture of herself with you at the party; she keeps it on her altar, what I call her altar: scented candles and all her jewelry. That picture, and a picture of her brother. And then Blister said he knew where you lived, and that you lived with a dancer."

"My husband's a writer."

"Your husband's Asian?"

"No. He's American."

"I guess Blister got the wrong idea," she said. "He said he ran into your husband in Chelsea. That he was on the way to dance practice?"

"Not my husband." I thought for a minute. "Blister knows where I live?"

"Yup, because his sponsor's some seminary guy. He was over there for lunch, and the seminary whatsit told him who was on the block, and you were, and some actor, was it some model?"

"I wonder why he didn't ring the bell."

"I don't know. But he did run into this guy who claimed he was your husband, and he was pulling a big box along?"

I suddenly understood. The only thing I didn't understand was why Kim would have said he was my husband.

"That guy visits somebody who lives in the building," I said. "He's trouble. Blister should stay away from him."

"It seemed odd to me. I told Blister I didn't believe it, because Blister picks up on zero, right? The guy wanted—it doesn't matter, since he's not your husband . . . the guy sort of asked him if he'd be interested in a threesome."

I put both hands on the edge of the table and looked at her.

"I told him that was bullshit," she said. "Not that it's wrong, or anything, if that's what you're into. It's not like he sees his sponsor there, usually. The sponsor had a broken foot, so he got Blister to come down, and they had a picnic or something out behind the place. And when Blister was leaving, he saw this guy who flirted with him, and he'd come out of your house, so—"

"We only rent the top floor. There are quite a few tenants in the building."

"Oh. I thought you might have been like us, because that's what everybody said—you'd been like us, but you went straight and figured out a way to get rich."

"People talk about other people, and they make things up. Then it becomes real to them. But it doesn't have anything to do with the other person."

Food was brought by the owner and a younger man from the kitchen, who pointed at the plates: "Manicotti. Insalata mista. Bread, just baked. No meat." The owner smiled broadly, poured water in our glasses, squeezed Destiny's shoulder, and left.

"He's nice, but he's not speaking to his daughter," she said, when they walked away.

"I lost my best friend when I got married," I said. "She didn't think my husband was worthy."

"Well, you're very cool," she said. "Is he?"

"He's sort of a Svengali."

"I don't know what that means."

"It means someone who's manipulative. More than that: somebody who makes you think you need him in order to accomplish anything."

"Your *husband*?"

"I'm on to him," I said. "I realized he was acting the way he did because he was insecure. What I was drawn to were the other parts of him: his brilliance; his spontaneity. I'd say his sense of humor, but every woman is deluded into thinking whoever she's with has a superior sense of humor. It's a way women approve of themselves."

"You live with a guy you think manipulates you?"

"No, I live with a guy who'd like to have that power, but who's lost it."

"And you'd tell me if it was the guy who wanted the threesome, right?"

"Destiny: that's *not* my husband."

"So what are you working on?"

I was silent for a while. The image of Kim dropping his robe on the floor popped up in my mind. The sash, streaming away. My copy editing work had dried up. I couldn't think of anything I'd done in a long time, so I lied; I pretended the research I'd done for Neil was more current. "I've been at the library researching birds of the South," I said. "As a favor to Neil. He had a contract—well, he decided it was too academic, but he had a contract to write about Southern writers, like Flannery O'Connor, and the use of birds in their work. When you talk about what you've turned up in your research it always sounds esoteric."

"I don't know what that word means."

"It means something only a few particular people would understand."

"Give me a chance. What did you find out about birds?"

"They're all different."

She continued to look at me expectantly.

"Take turkey buzzards: they're so big, they take off very slowly. They're vulnerable because of their weight. Clumsy. Sometimes easy prey. They have a highly developed sense of smell, and they ride the wind, looking for anything that might be, you know, dead."

"Carnivorous," she said, proud to let me know she knew the word.

"Neil, Neil, Neil. Do you miss locking eyes, moving your lips up my ear, whispering? You could do it all again, it just wouldn't have any power."

"Listen to yourself. These are the remarks you make, pulling on one of my T-shirts, thumping down on the bed, at one in the morning."

"If you've really reformed, don't you sort of hate yourself? Because what would you be? Some middle-aged guy who goes off to work and writes in a room papered with gold fleur-de-lys wallpaper some gay guys rent out?"

"You're acting like you think New York is a sane place."

"You're not listening. If you don't want to think about

yourself, how about me? You used to do an awful lot of thinking about how to educate me, before you'd convinced me what things of quality I could have a taste for, or acquire, to be a more sophisticated person. Now I drink Earl Grey tea—*loose* tea—and wear a Burberry raincoat with the belt tied in the back, and go to the tailor. I sleep on five-million-thread-count sheets, but I'm a reverse snob. I drink Prosecco instead of champagne. I get it, and there's no going back. You have plenty of money to support my desires, which are conveniently *your* desires."

"You don't think there was an electrical charge between us the minute we met?"

"We were both in dead-end relationships."

"Don't talk in clichés. Also: if you put this many duvets on the bed, why don't you sleep under them?"

"There are only two. Throw one off if you're hot. Feel my head."

"Jesus!" he said. "You're burning up."

"Flu."

"Flu? We had flu shots. Are you serious?"

"What do you think? I soaked in near boiling water, then came to bed?"

"We had flu shots."

"With inoculation, the flu will lack severity."

"What the hell!" he said. "Have you been talking to me while you're delusional? Where's the thermometer?"

"We don't have a thermometer. I didn't know which brand was the only brand to buy."

"Don't be a bitch just because you're sick."

"But you have an opinion, don't you? On which thermometer is best?"

"A 'bible'?"

"Right. Think of it as an *outline* of a TV show," my agent said.

"If I write the bible, what happens?"

"It gets approved, we hope. They make a pilot. Jonas says he has a lot of clout right now. The thing is, he needs it in a hurry."

"I don't know—"

"I'll messenger over some samples. But think wives. Waiting. Their daily life, the way they grow close, some become more patriotic, others don't, somebody gets breast cancer. Somebody gets pregnant by the roofer. You know. Children everywhere, always having to take care of the children."

"I wouldn't know—"

"Listen, it is a fabulous kill fee."

"Greetings, Jane. Though we never met, I get in touch with you and express my sympathy about Ben's passing and, to offer you some baby pictures if you would like them, perhaps in exchange for some memento from his more recent life such as a book that meant something to him or a paperweight, or also perhaps a pipe or something like that, if he smoked one. As children we made toys out of pipe cleaners and twisted them into various shapes such as eyeglasses which would also be nice to have as a remembrance of Ben. I visited Vermont one time but you were not there at that time. I appreciate, night skies with many stars. I will always remember my brother and the times we had in, for instance Vermont. If you ever find yourself in Sandusky please call and I hope you have pleasant memories of the person I loved so much as I do, and wish you well. With personal regards, Johnlene."

"Where's your robe, Kim?"

"That? I threw it out. Bottle blondes in Hollywood wear that trash. Faggots who wear mascara."

Neil and I were in a coffee shop in Chelsea, after seeing a show at the Guggenheim. Neil reached across the table and took my hand and narrowed his eyes—it was the way he punctuated important moments, as if time were a vowel he could elongate simply by staring.

He seemed nervous, though, which got my attention; almost like a young man about to propose. I was used to his whispering, which he did to create intimacy—even though I'd told him I was on to him—and which he also did as a way of communing with himself, or mocking the illusion that he was.

He reached across the table for my hand. "What I'm about to say is going to come as a surprise, but because I love you, I have to tell you. I want you to accept it, but I don't have any control over that. I won't be able to answer any questions, whatever you ask. Don't look at me that way. It's going to be all right. I've loved you, and I always will. But I'm going to disappear."

From the way he said it, I knew he wasn't kidding. His eyes were almost squeezed shut.

"Do you really think I'm going to accept that?" I said.

"I know what I *want* you to do," he said. "Think about it: would it have been easier if you'd gotten up and found a note? Would you want to think you'd been married to a coward?"

"This doesn't happen," I said. "People don't get married, then . . ."

I stopped, because of course it did happen.

"Who is it?" I said. "It's someone I don't know about at all, isn't it?"

"Nobody else. In an hour"—he looked at his watch—"more like half an hour, I'm going to get in a car. You can watch me get in, if you want, but that will break both our hearts. A lawyer is going to call you at five." He paused. "A *different* lawyer—not anyone either of us used drawing up the pre-nup." He said the term sneeringly. "The lawyer doesn't know where I'm going, but he knows what he's supposed to do. His name is Richard Flager. Everything I have is yours, including my heart. You're going to be fine."

"Did you kill somebody?" I said.

"Shhh," he said. "I love you, and I thank you for our life together."

There was no possibility he was kidding. None.

In such moments, very unrelated thoughts can occur to someone. In my case, I remembered an angry phone call from long ago as if it had just happened, in which my stepfather tried to persuade me to attend my college graduation for my mother's sake, and I had hung up screaming. I could still feel the scream, but not remember its sound. It was definitely the last time I had ever made such a noise. Now, I was not entirely optimistic about being able to speak again.

Time passed, but his eyes never widened, and never stopped looking into mine. His expression was very recognizable. I remembered the term Negative Capability, his little lecture standing at the stoplight. Keats's frozen figures. The transvestite zooming into the park. Neil blinked. It seemed for a few seconds that he might be on the verge of crying, but he was simply looking at me with the same eyes he had always trained on mine, in which I could see kindness, interest, perhaps even love. Quite possibly, love.

I thought about how I would stand up. I knew how to do that, of course, but we were in a booth, and sliding across the seat was not going to work because my legs had become numb.

"Where is this car going to come?" I said, looking away from his eyes, which had contained kindness, interest, and probably love.

"To the apartment," he said, and it was the last thing he ever said to me.

"Why the fuck does she care about some trashy robe? She went through the garbage? You two want the robe back? I can't believe this. And you think I'm the crazy one? It was shoplifted from Bloomie's. It wasn't your daddy's money that bought me the robe. It was my robe, and I divested. I wear a serape now. I'm not Jean Harlow. I'm a man who wears a serape."

Months passed, and my agent called, trying to jolly me into writing: "The world is waiting." Irony always exerted a persuasive pull. I felt better when it was present, like stacked duvets, even if it was necessary to turn some back for a while. That spring, the building went co-op, and I bought the fourth floor. Raymond, the psychologist, moved, as did the writer for the *Village Voice*. (He'd been living with another model in NoHo, anyway: eventually, he married her in a Buddhist ceremony in Mustique). Etch and Kim had a huge fight, followed by a commitment ceremony in P'Town, where I was the ring bearer: for the groom, a white gold band, set with onyx and a half-carat, channel-set canary diamond; for the bride, a Tiffany mesh bracelet fashioned into a jockstrap.

Blood oranges. (And also the novel, by John Hawkes.)

Rain. (And also the poem, by Robert Creeley.)

"*Stella!*" (And also the Italian cookies: crumbly Stella D'oro.)

I sometimes play a little game and think of myself as "Jane." It's a good game, because it really does give you some distance from yourself, and it lets you sort out what's important and what's not. If a character named Jane does this or that, you are only a kind of reporter. And you can report on something any number of ways.

Flashback: Jane and Neil are at a restaurant with a magazine editor, who is urging wine on them. What's the point of having her job if she doesn't make use of the expense account ha-ha-ha. Neil raises the glass to swirl the shallow liquid—the red of fluorescent-tinged puddles at night. It has started to rain, streaking the restaurant window. He takes a sip, nods. "Fine," he says, a bit querulously. (Is the waiter hyperalert to mixed messages—is that why he hesitates before he pours, first into Jane's glass, then the editor's, then—very tentatively—into Neil's?)

Jane is accepting a compliment from the editor. She picks up her stemmed glass of Côtes du Rhône. Later, she will be informed by Neil that she should ask for wine in "a short glass." The cocktail napkin sticks to the bottom. Later, he will tell her to discard them, because they are always (a word he likes to avoid in most cases so that when he does use it, it has great emphasis) only a hindrance. She will remember this all her life—both when it seems appropriate to the circumstances, and when such knowledge would not seem to apply. She will always remember this and always push away the cocktail napkin.

What sort of information is this for getting through life?

Extremely good information, she decides. He is dead (make that "dead")—the insurance company has investigated, though they have not yet closed the case.

She is set to inherit several million dollars from his life insurance policy, as well as the money she has already withdrawn from the bank account, and stock—some of which she has cashed in—that was bought during their brief marriage, after the sale of property in Sonoma. This wonderful, generous man—and she had once signed a pre-nup for which she consulted her own (her stepfather's) attorney! That wife, that aggressive wife . . . wouldn't you think she'd resurface after his death? But she doesn't.

Raymond left New York in October to run a boutique hotel in Miami Beach that has no sign, and an unlisted phone number.

Etch and Kim fought about whether to go to Italy on a vacation they couldn't afford.

All facts that could be flashed on the screen at the end of the movie. But there is no movie. Jane remembers those years, though, as if they had been—in part because her friends (who dwindled to only those people in the building) always talked about everything as if it was over ("Remember last night?"), while holding out the possibility that whatever happened could be rerun. Neil didn't have that sense of things. He thought people shouldn't romanticize ordinary life. "Our struggles, our little struggles," he would whisper, in bed, at night. Sometimes he or she would click on some of the flashlights and consider the ceiling, with the radiant swirls around the bright nuclei, the shadows like opened oysters glistening in brine. (In the '80s, the champagne was always waiting.)

Jane is driving north to Vermont: rental car, white Toyota Corolla, whizzing up the Merritt Parkway. She's listening to Chet Baker on the radio, wondering how someone with so little talent, so clearly only seductive, could have become so famous.

She stops to get gas and pee. The restroom smells of ammonia, and in the next stall, a woman is trying to hush her crying child.

Hours pass. She stops one more time, sits in a booth and has coffee. She remembers the red vinyl seat at the coffee shop in New York—a place she has never returned to, actually fearing it, as if it were the site of a real disaster. She thinks about Ben, in the hallway, with his pamphlets. Etch, saying something sarcastic about her taste in men.

Jane is not doing something sensible. She intends to try to rid herself of the memory of two men, though. The only person she told about this plan—Etch— agrees she should try something.

She drives and drives, and eventually gets to the house she lived in with Ben and sees the driveway, now paved, with a gate off its hinges and one upright, one leaning column. There is a FOR SALE sign. She pulls in, takes a deep breath, and opens the car door, gets out, and walks into the backyard.

The ring of phlox—her cutting garden—has disappeared. It is all scrubby lawn. She decides not to peek into the 4 x 4 windows of the house, but she likes the way they seem more like mirrors reflecting the sun than real windows. A nice quality of old glass. (As she wanders around, she is being watched by a security camera, but does not know it. The man who owns the property is cautious; there is an arsonist—who cares if it can't be proven?—two towns over.) The rosemary bush is gone—Vermonters always say they'll make it through the winter and sometimes they do, but not several consecutive winters. The azalea is spindly; the peach tree has grown. She walks around clumps of mud, clumps of grass, rock.

What happened to the family Ben told her about? She looks back at the gate.

(The man who owns the property looks at the wall monitor, says, "Damn," and lowers the footrest of his La-Z-Boy. He calls for his wife.)

It is terribly inappropriate, but Jane has not been able to think where to scatter Neil's ashes—of course, there was no trace of him when he was declared "dead," but she and Etch decided something symbolic needed to be done ("You two are ridiculous!" Kim shouted at them, before rushing out of the apartment), so Jane and Etch burned some of Neil's papers, and one of his shirts, in Etch's fireplace. They are in a Tiffany box, a blue Tiffany box, that once contained a cut-glass vase Neil gave her to hold the flashlight bouquet. Crazy, all of it, in retrospect, but it's the life she had. She has convinced herself that the ashes in the box represent Neil, and thinks he might like to be freed. She's weary, not concentrating on where she's walking, and almost twists her ankle in a gopher hole.

It was Ben she lived with here in Vermont, but part of her feeling sentimental has resulted in her notion that in some way, all men you love become similar because of that fact.

("Where the fuck are you?" the man who owns the property yells, scaring the cat. The La-Z-Boy is a piece of shit. He can tell from the way the footrest flapped down that it isn't going to come up again. Where is his wife when he needs her? Is he supposed to get in the truck and drive over to the property himself, with his bad foot?)

Two completely different human beings, Ben and Neil. Still, she imagines that if she gathers up something belonging to Ben, even if it is ground he walked on, her act may set them both free. This probably *is* pretty crazy, but who's to know? Only Etch, who adores her no matter what.

She turns away from the house—it is cold; she wraps her scarf around her neck—and tries to transport herself to Chelsea, to the golden oak bed, but she remembers, instead, the way it felt sleeping on Jan's floor, the hard wood under the sleeping bag, the two weeks she spent there that felt like two years, and she is overwhelmed with guilt that she stayed so long.

The heat at Jan's went off before eight, and didn't hiss on again until after 10 a.m. Where might Jan be? She hopes somewhere warm.

She paws the grass with her boot. Clever Hans. Does she instinctively understand signals from others and respond the way people want? Was that what was going on with Neil?

She read in the obits that Dr. Fendall died of cancer.

Adjacent to the property, there had been a row of boarded-up town houses. And the conflicting signs: DO NOT ENTER. FOR SALE. Meaning what? *Don't come in here, but if you look it over, you might want it?*

Who gets to go back? Nobody.

She's a little anxious because she's been trying to remember details of the journey to Ben's farm, and she can't remember stopping for gas, or anything she saw while driving. Well, she remembers trees, but nothing very specific. Other cars. The traffic thinning. The change in the air. She remembers a child crying in a restroom, and the child's mother trying to comfort it. As for the rest of the drive, she might pretend, mention big trucks when she tells the story to Etch, but she doesn't really remember passing anyone, or being passed.

Right before she got married, she had done what her stepfather suggested, and called an attorney who was a friend of his in Washington, who'd had the surname Prettyman.

When they first met, Neil had said: "It's not about having things figured out, or about communicating with other people, trying to make them understand what you understand. It's about a chicken dinner at a drive-in. A soft pillow. Things that don't need explaining."

"You never told me what your favorite movie was," she'd once said to him.

Then he disappeared. Not melodramatically, that second, but soon thereafter.

His favorite movie had been *Blowup*.

Now, having spent another day of the rest of her life alone, she is standing in a field in Vermont. She's driven a long way to realize that she has no vivid memories of her life inside the house, or outside the house, or even of the time she'd seen Ben in New York. Or, rather, standing outside the house they'd lived in, it is not revealed to her that anything means more than it does.

Jane is sitting on the ground, clutching her knees.

"Something I can do for you?" a woman bouncing

over the lawn in a Jeep calls out, her big forearm leaning out the open window, a red cap on her head.

"I used to live here," she says.

"So did I," the woman says, "in one of those houses down by the road, before the whole thing went belly-up. Now we live in a trailer."

They consider each other. Jane wonders if she will be asked about the blue box on the ground beside her.

"My husband picked you up," the woman says. At first, Jane does not understand.

"That's a monitor on that shutter," the woman says, pointing. "So you been auditioning for my husband, who must have kept looking, thinking you might do a lap dance." She laughs, amused with herself.

Jane is not entirely sure she believes the woman, but perhaps it's true. Perhaps she has been observed. Who can see as far as the shutter?

"My husband said somebody was checking it out to break in. I thought it would be somebody who had an eye on the antiques in advance of the auction."

"I don't know anything about that."

"Maybe there's something that would strike your fancy. I've got the key." The woman points to a cluster of things dangling from the truck's rearview mirror.

"It doesn't . . . I don't think it would make me feel better to go inside," she says.

The woman nods. "It's private property, marked DO NOT ENTER, and my husband's in a bad mood today."

"I'll be leaving."

"New York plates. You drove from there? To look things over and drive back?"

"Memory lane."

The woman brushes her hair out of her eyes. "Anything you'd want to share?"

"It was a long time ago. The town houses weren't put up. When we lived here, the old farmer and his wife were alive. Ben rented, and worked on the land."

"You know Goodness?" the woman says, her voice suddenly changing.

"I did. He died."

"What do you mean, died?"

"He died. There was . . . it was an accident, in New York."

"Fuck!"

"I'm sorry."

"A car accident?"

"That's the general idea. I'd appreciate it if I didn't have to talk about it right now."

"Waaaaaait a minute," she says. "Are you the girl-friend?"

Jane nods.

"I heard about you. My brother-in-law met you one time, Dwight? He built the tennis courts. He said one night you three played Monopoly in a big snow-storm. He's bankrupt. I heard about you when I hung out with Goodness after you left, back when I was in high school. He taught me to park so I could pass my driver's test. I can't believe he's dead, that doesn't make any sense. Are you here to dig up the time capsule?"

"What?"

"I'm not dumb just because I live in Vermont."

"What?" Jane says again.

"I'm not gonna stop you! I was worried about what was going to happen to it, because the tree's half dead. Whoever buys the property will probably take it down. Of course, if the bank repossesses it, they're too stupid to take down a half-dead tree." She is big-hipped, in jeans that end above her ankle. She is wearing thick white socks. There is a wedding ring on her puffy finger.

"Nancy Drew stuff, right?" she says, striding past Jane.

Jane catches up, and falls into step. "A lot of things happened after we broke up," she says. "I married somebody else, and he just died too."

"Do you have any good luck? That's what Dwight says to me: 'Got any good luck to tell me?' He'll be watching both of us, bored to death but too lazy to come over here and see what's up. What do I care if he knows about the time capsule?"

They walk. It is as if the blue box isn't even there. How will she scatter Neil's ashes? What, exactly, was her initial idea?

"My name's Cora," the woman says.

"Jane," Jane says. "Where we're walking, there used to be a bed of phlox."

"I remember. All died from mildew. Those other people who came after Ben left, they thought it was a sin to pick flowers! I'd come with my pruning shears and that woman would have herself a heart attack, worried to death I might be committing a sin. They didn't last the winter. Speaking of the phlox back there, that wouldn't have been a good place to bury the capsule. Bad drainage."

"Where are we going?"

"Stop pretending. That tree, over where the woods start."

"Will anything convince you I don't know what you're talking about?"

"Not if you're *here*. It's not a big deal, I saw what was in it, it's not like it's a million dollars. Hey, if it was, don't you think I'd be out of here, living in Florida?"

"Let's leave it where it is, whatever it is. I don't think I'm going to be able to deal with this."

"It's my responsibility to give it to you so it won't be destroyed."

The tree's trunk is partly hollow. Three boards nailed to the tree form rickety steps. A fourth swings free, having slipped a nail. The others are high off the ground; you'd need a ladder to climb them, and you still wouldn't get anywhere near the top.

"You know, this is going to sound really strange, but

I brought a box with me of my husband's ashes. To scatter somewhere beautiful. Like in the woods. That's what's in that blue box back there."

"None of my business," the woman says. She kicks aside some leaves and lifts out a brick from the hollow of the tree. In the distance, a dog begins barking. She digs where the brick was with a stick and then with her hand. "Not such a good job burying it," she says. "You know what? I do believe my husband's lost sight of us, but you know what else? He'll go back to his chair and take a nap, that's what." She stops rummaging and holds out a brown rectangle the size of a cigarette pack, but thinner. It has two rusted clamps, one on each side, and a cord that's mostly deteriorated. She wipes the dirty rectangle on her jeans, as if she's polishing an apple. She flips up the clamps and extends her hand.

Inside is a folded piece of paper that turns out to be a photocopy of the famous picture of the sailor kissing the nurse in Times Square on V-J Day, though now there is a cut-out photograph of her face where the nurse's face had been. Above it, in a hand-drawn heart, is written: *Ben and Jane 1979–1980.*

It's like something a child would make, more curious than moving. Something rattles in the rectangle: a cheap ring you'd get from a vending machine. "I wore it on my pinkie before he put it in," the woman says.

"You did? An engagement ring?"

"Noooooo, it's a mood ring. I put it on and it turned pink, so that meant it was love. He wasn't really in love with me, but I had a crush on him and we made out a little bit. Just fooling around."

"He buried this?"

"I told him to. I bought it at a flea market. He liked it, but he didn't want to take a present from me until I explained it could be a time capsule. There should be a pill in there, too."

"Cyanide?" Jane says, amused.

Jane turns the pack over. Nothing falls into the palm of her hand. The woman takes it back and peers inside. "It got crapped up," she says. "I see it down there. It was one of those pills you drop in water, and it unfolds into a flower. If he ever got you back, you'd put on the mood ring, and he could be really romantic and grow you a flower." Cora looks at the ground. "I was just a kid," she says. "Stop looking at me like I'm retarded."

"What should I do with this?" Jane says, tucking the piece of paper back inside.

"I knew one day we'd meet. Of course, I didn't know you'd come here to tell me he was dead. I'm just as glad it's some other guy's ashes, not his. Goodness's ashes blowing around would make me pretty sad." Cora looks away, into the trees. "It wasn't anything but fooling around," she says, "and also, it was a long time ago."

"I've got to get going," Jane says.

"The key's in the truck if you want to go in. I know I keep saying that, but I can't believe you don't want to."

"No thanks."

"The furniture's got tags on it. The flower pictures are already sold. It might make you sad, I guess. I'd go in sometimes and lie on the bed and dream I was the butterfly flying over the rose, or the moth in the moonlight. He brought back a whole box of them. I never asked where he got them. He had a romantic streak. Not that I saw much of it." Cora looks straight into Jane's eyes. She says: "Do you want to stay here by yourself and pray?"

"No thank you. I'm not religious."

"There's a bean supper at the firehouse tonight, if you're staying around."

"I have to get back. But thanks for mentioning it."

"So you got married, and your husband died, too? You're pretty young to be a widow. That must be rough."

"Life's unpredictable."

"I guess so. Nothing ever showed up on Dwayne's security camera but squirrels and birds, and every now and then a deer walking through. Then here you come, and I'm supposed to be the one to confront you."

Jane holds out her hand. "Well. Nice to meet you, Cora."

"Likewise." Cora's hand is rough; Jane can barely

feel bones through the puffiness. "There's a gun in my truck, but I never thought of using it once I looked at your face," Cora says, with a big smile.

Jane's eyes grow wide.

"I'll be going, so you can have your privacy," Cora says. "If it's not too personal, how come that box is bright blue? Was that his favorite color, or something?"

"Oh, it's . . ." Jane does not want to say it is a box she took down from the top of her closet. So she says yes, and I realize, as she does, that I never knew Neil's favorite color.

Etch opened his door when I came into the hallway.

"Depressing, or okay?"

"Some weird woman drove up and never stopped talking. I didn't scatter his ashes there. I ended up at a park in Pound Ridge."

"I didn't quite get the significance of scattering his ashes where you and that other guy lived, myself. Want to come in for tea?"

"You know, I don't think I could contend with Kim right now."

"He's at the movies with some Filipino he's got a crush on," Etch said. He looked at his watch. "For another hour, minimum."

I went in and sank onto the sofa.

"Green, black, or decaf?" he said.

"Actually, I'd like some Jack Daniel's, if you have it."

"He drank it all. I have a six-pack of Corona, though."

"Corona," I said.

"I know our relationship's been strained," he said, opening a drawer in the galley kitchen. "I think I've already told you that I think his sense of humor is inappropriate a lot of the time. You should only meet the Filipino." Two bottle caps popped off. "He does what he thinks is a hilarious imitation of Ed McMahon. It comes over him every time he sits on the sofa. The first few times, I thought he was just talking to himself, another psycho."

"What does he say?"

"He chortles. He expects everybody else is mentally filling in the Johnny Carson part."

"Thank you," I said, taking the bottle. He clinked his to mine and sat across from me in the velvet butterfly chair.

"This strange woman in Vermont was who?"

"The wife of the developer, who's gone bankrupt. She dug a little box she called a 'time capsule' out from inside a tree. It doesn't matter. You're right. It wasn't the right place to scatter his ashes."

"Did you call that guy? The postman?"

"No. I completely forgot."

"That's too bad. He's been so loyal, sending you

postcards with news of the town. Would you like some pretzels?"

"No thanks."

"Could you maybe say that everything's fine between us, even though Kim is an asshole?"

"Everything's fine. Don't worry about it."

"I had a talk with him last night and he made it pretty clear he's not leaving me for the Filipino, it's just about sex. I guess I believed him."

"You could do a million times better."

"Straight people always romanticize the romantic potential of queers."

A police siren started outside. A dog barked through it, and continued after it ended.

"Another friend's come down with that gay cancer," he said.

"Really? A good friend?"

"More his than mine," he said. He looked toward the window. "Oh, bark, bark, bark," he said. "Yip, yip, yip, yip, yip. By the way, my father's written me out of his will, but he's being magnanimous and not evicting me. He's leaving everything to my sister in Hattiesburg. She remembered to send him a birthday card."

I kept in contact with Etch when I left New York. He moved to a different building. His father threw him out, after all. He volunteered as a counselor at the Gay Men's Health Alliance and worked at a men's clothing store in the old neighborhood, which began getting very gentrified. He adopted a mutt and named him Etch, which caused no confusion because when I left, he started going by his given name, Harold.

I moved into a rented farmhouse in Virginia and spent the next year writing the book on which the movie *La Seule Vacance* was based. My novel, as you might know, was titled *The Only Time We Went Away*. Much of the writing came directly from Neil's notebooks: his observations, his frustration at his inability to express the extent of his love for me (which I had begun to think was deliberate. Writing about it in the notebooks, I mean, knowing I'd find them). I made my character a writer—different from Neil in some ways, but guided by Neil's information: as he always told me, the French love to think Americans are crazy, and therefore that all American novelists are crazy. We think theirs are sulky; they think ours are a bunch of Maileresque hotheads. The reviews, in the U.S., called the Neil I'd created "a *Saturday Night Live* Svengali" and "Dr. Doolittle Deconstructed." The character was "as menacing in his intentions as Jack Nicholson in *The Shining*." This was a different take than the French had on the film—though I hadn't meant it to be anywhere near as funny as they found it. (Which might also express the innermost thoughts of Jerry Lewis, I suppose.) The film, and the book's subsequent translation into French, provided a great launching pad for the sale of my next novel, for which I also wrote the screenplay—though, in true Hollywood fashion, it didn't go anywhere the minute Meryl Streep signed on for another project.

"It was good to hear from you after so long. Are you really still worried that you overstayed your welcome in my crappy little apartment? It's true I had to nudge you out, but I enjoyed having you there for a while. It's just that you never had any sense you were imposing, so I didn't think sleeping in a sleeping bag was ever going to get to you. I knew you'd never offer to split the rent—I knew you were going to end up fine and I wasn't, that was clear from the beginning. If you want to blame yourself for something, what about all the take-out food you never chipped in on? You always just sailed through situations, and that used to really bug me. Everything's different since I survived chemo. Now I only wish people the best, and if they're just expressing their nature, so be it. You didn't ask in your note how I was. It was nice to hear about you, about your books (haven't read them, I'll be honest), the house you recently purchased. If you *had* asked about me, I could honestly say I've just survived the worst year of my life. Anyway: onward and upward."

A final litany, before forgetting:

Invest in Disney.

Never take flowers to a dinner party. Send them beforehand. Also, if you receive flowers, never leave the card out. To everyone else, the sender has to remain a mystery.

When you travel to Europe, never wear a fragrance from the country you're in. In France, wear perfume made in Italy.

Have sex in airplane bathrooms.

If you can't stand on your head, which is best, learn to do cartwheels.

Look out for any man who wears more jewelry than a watch. A pocket watch, out of sight, is best. Never have anything to do with a man who has a watch fob.

Don't have flowers in the house that refer to any myth people might know. No hyacinths. No narcissus.

Never miss a solar eclipse.

Read all of Turgenev and enough Proust to say you've read more than you have, so people won't nag you.

Notice who the cinematographer is. In the future, see movies based on that.

Wear only raincoats made in England.

Screen calls. Never answer the phone when it rings. It's only an indication that someone wants to talk to you.

What all men think, that's different from all women, is that they're going to the stars.

Don't use the year of your birth for your cash machine code. Use the numbers that correspond to the first four letters of your astrological sign. If you're a Leo, double the "o."

When depressed, look at Halsman's photographs of people jumping, especially the Duchess of Windsor.

Time changes everything. (Best sung by Merle Haggard.)

Years after I'd left New York, and shortly after I found out my mother died (we had rarely talked on the phone the last few years of her life), I made a second trip to see my stepfather, Carl, in Lexington. He'd moved in with an old army buddy, a widower, to a house in town, where he gardened and belonged to various do-good organizations. We'd never had a close relationship because he'd married my mother the same year I went to college, and he was older, a conservative, so guarded in what he said about homosexuals that it was clear to me he was homophobic. I suspected that in recent years he'd become more of a drinker. He had always been kind to me, though, from arranging for me to see the specialist in New York back when I'd been living with Ben in Vermont and had had my yearlong stomachache, to calling me often after my mother died, to see how I was doing. He'd had a review of my novel, from the Roanoke paper, enlarged and laminated. He sent it to me by UPS, with a gold star pinned to the top. When I called Etch and told him about the gift, he joked that I could hold it horizontally and use it the way Gypsies do, dancing around to distract tourists outside the train station in Rome, while their children pick the tourists' pockets.

Carl came down the walkway, waving and carrying a pan of what turned out to be burned brownies in his other hand. The oven mitt had transformed his hand into an enormous lobster claw.

"The writer!" he said. "And looking especially nice today."

When he kissed my cheek, I smelled vodka. I waited while he dumped the burned food into the trash. "Have to be careful, get the lid down tight, the raccoons around here just walk up and toss the cans over," he said.

We went into the house. It was a Victorian, with high ceilings and stacks of pictures on the walls. Stanley collected old, hand-colored photographs.

"Good to see you," Stanley said, rising from his

chair. He'd been reading the newspaper. The house smelled strongly of burned food. He stepped forward and shook my hand.

"I have something I wish you'd help me with, Carl," he said immediately, wandering into the kitchen. Carl and I followed. The problem was a box of tea, shrink-wrapped. Stanley had not noticed the plastic and couldn't figure out how to get it open.

"A couple of old duffers," Carl said. "But we do okay."

"Candle snuffers?" Stanley said.

"Duffers. Old *duffers*," Carl repeated.

"We're thinking about a smaller house, less upkeep. Not a bad time to buy," Stanley said. "I'm donating my collection to the college. Then there's going to be an auction of some furniture next month."

Stanley seemed a little unsteady on his feet as he filled the teakettle. "Lost our kettle," he said. "Took it outside to water, forgot it was there, and it got lifted up by that storm we had and blew right into the neighbor's car. Made a big dent in the door. Ruined the kettle, too." He shook his head. "This is a junk store special," he said. "Boils water as well as the next thing."

"But it's almost dinnertime. Won't you let me take you to dinner?" Carl said. "Stanley, we could all three do with a good meal. A glass of wine, instead of tea?"

"Well now, the problem there is that I've got to take

my walk for my blood pressure, and I haven't done that yet."

"I'd like to stretch after driving," I said. "Can we go with you on your walk?"

"Don't see why not. Walking's good at any age," Stanley said. "I might look for my moccasins and do the Daniel Boone. My left heel could feel better." His front tooth was chipped. There was a little dried blood above his lip, where he'd nicked himself shaving. He examined himself in the hall mirror. "Haven't seen my shoes, have you, Carl?"

"I don't believe I have."

"Well, if I was Ricky Ricardo, this might be the start of something funny," he said, going up the stairs.

"Do you still watch 24?" I asked Carl.

"Wouldn't miss it. Every week, Bauer saves the world."

"Put that young man on Omaha Beach, we'd get a better idea of what he could do, and couldn't do," Stanley called over his shoulder.

"I appreciate your coming for a visit on the eve of my birthday," Carl said. "And I was very happy to receive the subscription to *Harper's* magazine, as well. Thank you very much."

"You're welcome."

"Your mother's death is still quite a shock to me. But Stan and I do pretty well for a couple of old guys. We get along."

"How do you feel about selling the house?" I said.

"Probably a good time to put it on the market," he said, not answering the question. "You're driving back tonight?"

"It's not a long drive."

"I can't argue, after what Stan did the other time."

Stanley had loaned the neighbor his "extra mattress" for the collie to give birth; he later took it home and put it back on the box spring in the guest bedroom, where I spent the night, wondering what the strange smell was in the room.

"I'm over it," I said. "It was funny."

"Stan can get to thinking life goes along the way *I Love Lucy* does," he said. "We have a lovely inn in Lexington, you know." He had walked over to the big hall table, where many daguerreotypes were displayed in frames, along with silver bowls and copper pitchers. Stanley's shoes sat on top of the sideboard, thick with dried mud and leaves.

"Stanley!" he called. "Found your shoes."

We took a walk. We walked on the sidewalk, up the steep hill that went past the church, then turned onto a street where a friend of theirs lived. Stanley was taking the man a book. "Tells him what to do with fish rather than deep-fry it," he said.

Carl and I waited while he went up the walkway and left it in a basket outside the front door.

"Get to be our age, it would be downright unkind to knock at what might be naptime," he said.

Stanley straggled behind a bit, which was probably his notion of giving me time alone with Carl. Carl said: "Shortly before your mom died, a friend of yours from New York got in contact. Joan? No, Jan. Said you and Neil had broken up before the wedding, and she tried to keep you out of it, but you two both had your minds set on getting married, so there was nothing for it."

"Jan wrote to my mother?"

"She offered some information about a vitamin or something that makes the side effects of chemo better. I don't think it was the first time she'd written."

"She's only written to me once, in all these years. I wonder why she did that?"

"Don't know, but your mother appreciated the gesture."

"You think about her a lot?"

"Oh, I'm well aware that what happened was for the best."

"You mean, if she was going to drink herself to death, it was good she didn't have to go on kidney dialysis?"

He hung his head. He finally said, "The doctor told me the liver would go, so that wasn't such a shock."

"You took good care of her," I said.

"She would have done the same."

"But she didn't. She always created situations that made you take care of her."

"You and your mother didn't get along all that well.

Not every child does, just because someone's a parent. But she was always proud of you. Always happy for your success. Couldn't understand why you married that man who ran away, but it was none of our business."

"I don't think even if he'd stayed we were all destined to get along."

"How are you doing, yourself?" Carl asked.

"Fine."

"Did he do any military service?"

"What? No. He didn't."

"Why is that?"

"Maybe he had some medical problem."

"Maybe! You don't know?"

"We never talked about it."

"And that wife of his just went to Mexico and divorced him?"

"After getting a considerable financial settlement."

"I usually don't ask direct questions, because I don't believe it's polite, but just this once, out of idle curiosity, what would a 'considerable financial settlement' consist of, so an old fogey like me can be shocked?"

"Two million dollars, their condo, and her jewelry. I'm sure she would have gotten the car, but he didn't believe in buying cars."

Carl let out a long, slow whistle.

We came over a rise. In a leafless tree at the back of someone's property, turkey buzzards were roosting, weighing down the branches, flying up when more birds, streaming across the sky, landed. I had never before seen so many. They kept coming, an amazing number of them, circling in the darkening sky.

"Damn buzzards!" Stanley said. "Nothing stops 'em. They used to favor the tree by the Baptist church, and the minister would be out there, blasting an air rifle in the direction of God. That's the way he put it: 'Talking to God and begging him to get 'em to go away. Not firing to kill, just having a word with God.'" He smiled. "Looks like a tree in Hell. You could take a picture of that and show it to somebody and tell them that's what it's like, that's trees in Hell, no leaves, no Spanish moss dangling, no pink blossoms, *vultures.*"

"They're not," I said. "They're commonly assumed to be some kind of vulture, but they're really descended from storks, and ibis."

"Ibid?" Stanley said.

"Ibis," Carl repeated loudly.

"Well, that's a relief: if it was ibid, I guess I'd have to wonder what the hell that book had been!" Stanley said.

We walked past the antiques store. Three cadets from VMI came down the street. One was eating an ice cream cone.

"Your mother was a little jealous that you had such success and lived in New York," Carl said. "She used to say, 'Do you think if her name was up in lights she'd think she'd accomplished enough, and settle down and have a normal life?' "

"My mother was an alcoholic. I think she was more interested in drinking than in how her daughter turned out."

"Sorry. I shouldn't have told you that," Carl said.

We turned the corner. A tall man in a sports jacket, walking very upright, and a shorter, dark-haired man came toward us.

"Evening, Cy," Stanley called out behind us. "There's a Hieronymus Bosch painting waiting for you just around the bend."

"Maybe better to turn back and have a cocktail, then!" the dark-haired man said. He spoke with a strong Italian accent.

"Evening," Carl said, nodding as we passed.

These were the quick greetings of small-town people who crossed paths too often to really talk.

"What do you think of that—someone as famous as Cy Twombly, moving home from Italy for part of the year, back to his roots, I guess," Carl said.

Stanley caught up with us. "Cy, out for his evening stroll," he said. "Can you imagine if Ricky Ricardo came home with one of Cy's paintings and tried to put it on the wall? Can you imagine what Lucy would have to say about that?"

Carl gave me a look; Stanley was obsessed.

"That husband of yours," Stanley said. "Carl and

I were wondering: Did you ever think he might have gone into the witness protection program?"

"Stan!" Carl said.

"What? How many possibilities are there? Do you have a better idea?"

"I did think about that," I said. "He had some relatives who were pretty frightening. People I met just after we got married and never saw again. So you might be right, Stanley. Or he could have been like Gatsby, who went pretty far before he got shot in his swimming pool."

"Is that what happened to The Great Gatsby? Died in his pool?"

I nodded.

"Who shot him?" Stanley said.

"It's not entirely clear. He was in love with some other man's wife. His real name was Jay Gatz. He had some connection with criminals."

"You can never know a person," Stanley said. "Never know 'em any more than you can figure out their life story by looking at their photograph."

I had almost no photographs of Neil, even if I'd wanted to study them. He had an aversion to cameras, put his hand up if someone tried to photograph him, or even the park in which he sat. I had no photographs of our wedding party. But of course I had tried to figure things out, and I'd had written documents, information (as Neil would have pronounced the word)—misinformation, I eventually realized. Reading Neil's notebooks, I had slowly begun to understand that what I was reading was fiction. He thought up profound one-liners so he could seem to effortlessly drop them into conversations. He knew I'd find his notebooks—that was why he'd written, so often, about how much I meant to him. They weren't even hidden. He knew I would discover them in his desk drawer when he left.

His ashes had blown back at me. Comedy skits loved to joke about that. It repulsed and delighted people to think of such a thing happening: the wind lifting the ashes off the waves, blowing them back into the rowboat; the little gray clump that rolled like tumbleweed, getting caught under the survivor's heel. First his ashes had blown back—not even his ashes, of course; make-believe ashes for a make-believe person—and at that moment two boys had raced toward me on the path, one coming up too close and colliding with the other, both boys suddenly wailing on the ground, the boy pinned underneath with a broken nose, the boy on top with a broken thumb. Their father had come running, confused at first—seeing me bending over them, the blood on the ground. Blood speckling the empty Tiffany box. Of course he understood in a second that I was just another person out walking. Like Cora in Vermont, he realized I was harmless, a person carrying a box, for whatever reason, taking a walk.

"Maybe that husband turned into a buzzard," Stanley said. "Should we get the binoculars and go back and examine those fellows in that tree?"

"I don't know what's gotten into him," Carl said.

"I can hear you, you know," Stanley said, ruddy-faced, hair slick with sweat from the walk. "I'm right here beside you."

© Sigrid Estrada

About the Author

Ann Beattie has published seven novels and eight collections of stories. She has been included in four O. Henry Award collections and in John Updike's *Best American Short Stories of the Century*. In 2000, she received the PEN/Malamud Award for achievement in the short story form. In 2005, she received The Rea Award for the Short Story. She and her husband, Lincoln Perry, live in Key West, Florida, and Charlottesville, Virginia, where she is Edgar Allan Poe Professor of Literature and Creative Writing at the University of Virginia.